Kullman, Harry
The Battle horse

THE BATTLE HORSE

Translated from the Swedish
by George Blecher and Lone Thygesen-Blecher

THE BATTLE HORSE

BY HARRY KULLMAN

BRADBURY PRESS   SCARSDALE, NEW YORK

1 2 3 4 5   85 84 83 82 81

Library of Congress Cataloging in Publication Data
Kullman, Harry. The Battle Horse.
Translation of: Stridshästen.
Summary: The children on a Stockholm street engage in a
modern-day jousting tournament in which the rich are knights
and the poor are the horses who bear them.
[1. Social classes — Fiction. 2. Sweden — Fiction.
3. Play — Fiction]   I. Title.
PZ7.K949016Bat   [Fic]   81-2192
ISBN 0-87888-175-1   AACR2

THE BATTLE HORSE

1

The first time I saw the Black Knight from the Deepest Darkness with my own eyes was a hot, summery September afternoon.

In those days we lived in an old-fashioned backhouse, and even if it was still summer in September, in October it could change right over to winter. That's why I used to go down to Ostermalm Square to find wood; Mom felt that it didn't hurt to collect fuel for the oven and stove early, and besides, I needed boards and lumber for a soapbox racing car I was planning to build.

In a corner of the square near Sibyll Street there was a construction site where you could find really good boards. You could also look around in the big trash boxes where they put the broken stands and smashed fruit boxes from the market. With a little luck you might find some discarded plums, apples, and pears which you could eat if you cut away the

1

rotten parts. Or you could pinch fruit and vegetables off the stands on your way across the square. The square was always lively and bustling at dusk when the market people packed up for the day: buses chugged through the street that cut the square in half, old guys brawled in front of the beer cafes, and people rushed around to do some last minute shopping.

The people who owned the stands weren't exactly friendly to me and my friends. They chased us away the minute they had the chance. "Hey, you damn kids," they'd say, "what are you hanging around here for? Get lost!" One or two of them had trucks, but most just had ordinary handcarts, and you had to steal stuff from them before they loaded the stands, racks, boards, and boxes onto the carts: if they caught you pinching from the loaded carts, all hell would break loose.

Once a cop stopped me just as I was leaving the marketplace with a pile of boards under my arm.

"Hey, what have you got there? Where do you think you're going?"

"I got them on the square. I'm building a soapbox racer."

He didn't say anything, but he did look at me suspiciously before he nodded for me to take off. Grownups didn't like the idea that the boxes and boards were being used for firewood, but they didn't say anything if you said you were building a hut or a fort or a car. And I *was* building that car; I had a blueprint of it at home in the kitchen. It was going to have narrow straps for steering, and real brakes so that you wouldn't go flying into the inlet when you raced down Prince Street.

It was also going to have a Ford insignia in front, a real one. You see, I was a Ford man. Some of my classmates were Chevy men, and we used to fight each other during recess. The Ford men would bend over and butt the Chevy men, and the ones who could push the others over to the wall would win. "Ford is best!" we'd shout. "Ford *is* best!"

So I was planning to go to Ostermalm Square on that silky-smooth September afternoon. But when I got outside into the courtyard of our building, I heard Henning and Max talking about the Black Knight. I put my hands in my pockets and strolled slowly over to the tree—we had a tall, bushy oak in the middle of the yard, and it was against that, with their backs to the front house, that the two preppies in the building sat.

Preppies, that was our name for them, for all the kids who went to Ostra Prep. Of course, a lot of them went to even fancier schools like Almquist School on Artillery Street, but we called them preppies too—just as we did the girls at the Normal School.

A preppie was, you might say, a rich man's kid. They always lived in the front houses, which often had both central heating and bathrooms. They wore nice clothes and school caps with emblems on them. They ate at regular hours and even had their own rooms, and their mothers had cooks, nurses, and maids. Their fathers (you couldn't call those serious men with white shirts and starched collars dads) were rich and important—they were businessmen, judges, doctors.

The kids like us who went to public school used to brag among ourselves about the preppies and their fancy fathers, although I didn't really have to do it; everyone knew that Henning lived in my yard, and Henning's father was a general. If you could believe the rumors that we heard from the other preppies, Henning wasn't only best at all the subjects in school, he was best at *everything*: he was great at all the team sports, he ran the 60 meter hurdles in-record time in the All-Prep Track Meet, *and* he was a master at fencing and sharpshooting!

"I'm going to do the modern pentathlon and win a gold medal in the Olympics," he'd say, and no one doubted him.

There was another preppie in my yard—Max, a friendly kid. His father was a banker, though that was nothing to brag about. There were bankers and bank managers on almost every block in Ostermalm. Max was always nice; he chatted with me even in the street. With the other kids, you got the feeling— and some said they'd actually heard preppies say— that they weren't *allowed* to hang around with us ordinary kids.

"They probably think we're going to teach them how to curse. As if they didn't know already," said Olle, a restless, chubby classmate of mine, and a

4

Ford man like me. "The only difference between them and us is that they're too chicken to curse at home."

I didn't think that was the only difference. We took it for granted the preppies were smarter than us, that being richer kids they'd been given extra or better brains at birth.

"Well no," admitted Olle, "maybe it isn't the only difference. But people are more alike than you think. Maybe preppies brag too—not about us, but about our fathers."

"About our fathers? What for? They're nothing to brag about."

"That's the whole point! The preppies brag backwards, you might say. They think it's special to have a kid in the yard whose father has a really crummy job. Lawyers and professors, they're just shit to them. But *real* shit—that they love. Like my Pop for instance; he's a night carrier."

"What's that?"

"Didn't I ever tell you? He empties barrels of shit at night in the Old Town where they still have a lot of outhouses. What a stink that is!"

But I didn't believe that the preppies were one bit interested in our dads or their jobs. Least of all proud Henning, who condescended once in a while to say a word to me, but usually gave me only a cool nod. It was just impossible to imagine him saying, "There's a boy named Roland in our yard. Would you believe it—his father works in a factory!"

And in fact it really wasn't anything special. Factory workers were a dime a dozen in Ostermalm, just like bankers, though of course *we* lived in old-fashioned, run-down buildings.

The factory where my pop worked was called United Chocolate. A chocolate factory—didn't that sound promising? In practice, though, the security was so tight you couldn't even smuggle out a bar of chocolate. If you tried and they caught you, you'd get fired on the spot. My pop used to say, "Just wait till I'm foreman. They don't check the supervisors and foremen—they just nod to the guards and strut out on Rorstrand Street with their pockets *full* of the stuff."

Most of the time on Friday nights Mom and I would wait outside the factory to keep Pop from going off with Fat Fredrik to gamble and drink away his pay. I went along so that he'd have someone to blame it on when he tried to get away. Mom would stand at a little distance in the crowd so as not to embarrass him, but I'd trot right over to the gate. Then Pop could say to the pig-eyed Fredrik, "N-no thanks, I promised the kid to go to the game (or visit Uncle Anton or buy sneakers)." And afterwards Mom would bawl him out: "You've got to learn to say no," she'd say. "You don't have to go along with him like all those other idiots. All he wants is your money; everybody knows how those *Southerners* are."

But Pop couldn't say no to his pals, his work buddies, or his friends at the bar. He wanted them to think he was the world's best guy, and so they could

6

get him to go along with everything. Mom, on the other hand, didn't care one bit about the other workers' wives; she never took part in their gossip and morning coffees. But when one of the fancy ladies would speak to her, well, then she became a different person: she'd get all nervous-looking, and she'd be difficult to be around. She'd even talk differently; slang and swear words would just vanish. That was because she was probably thinking about the time one of the maids said she spoke just like an "educated" lady.

The general had spoken to her a few times, and that made her special among the women of the backhouse—which suited her just fine. For that matter, though, he'd even spoken to me. "Stand up straight, boy!" he'd commanded me once when I held the gate to the street open for him. It didn't feel very special to me.

But I understand how she felt. Just the fact that Henning's father was a general and Henning was the greatest of all the preppies rubbed off on me, it really did. I was looked up to just because Henning and I lived in the same yard.

Actually, the yard with its old oak tree *was* a little out of the ordinary. Some gnarled roots were sticking up from the ground, and they formed a hollow or pocket where you could sit with your back against the trunk. The cavity was big enough for two people; it had become Max and Henning's favorite place.

Now, sitting there, they both looked very suntanned. They'd been out in the archipelago all summer where their families had summer houses—Max on Runmar Island and Henning on Moja. I didn't envy them, though; as a matter of fact, I thought it was like being deported to be forced to stay in the country when you could explore Ostermalm all summer. Henning had visited Max during their vacation—the general liked to sail, and he'd let Henning hold the tiller when they crossed Kanholm Bay. "I'm going to get my own boat," Henning was saying. "A small version of the *Folk* boat. Clinker-built. Flat-stern. Cuddy-cabin." It was all strictly Greek to me; I felt flattened out by all his fancy words.

But then Max interrupted. "If anybody's going to beat the Black Knight in the tournament, it's you," he said. "Everybody thinks so."

2

Max and I would probably have been better friends if Henning hadn't been around. I got along well with Max—he was always warm and friendly. He loaned me exciting books, played marbles with me in the spring, and sometimes took his dartboard down to the yard where we'd nail it up on the wooden carpet airing rack and fool around with it.

"But the first order of business is to get a horse," Henning was saying to him.

I had a hard time with Henning. In some ways I wouldn't have minded being his best friend (like Max was), but at the same time I felt sort of envious because *I* wasn't Henning, wasn't "noble," didn't live in the front house, and wasn't best at everything. Henning was big, strong, and blond; at that moment his hair seemed almost white against his brown face. He held an oak leaf between his fingers and rolled it distractedly into a green cigarette.

"*Then* I'll defeat the Black Knight and win the whole tournament," he went on.

"You could use Roland," said Max.

It was the first time Henning turned to look at me. His nod was almost imperceptible, but I could hardly meet the sharpness of his gaze. I felt like he'd undressed me, read my thoughts, discovered my innermost dreams. No wonder I felt nervous around him.

"I'm too heavy for him," he finally decided.

It seemed to me that he hadn't even considered me as a possibility. And we could have at least *tried*. For even though I didn't really want to be his horse, I knew that horses made money—and for money I'd carry the heaviest load.

Olle had told me everything about the tournament and the Black Knight. He was the horse for a preppie from his courtyard on Grand Street and was paid by the preppie and given extra prize money every time his team won. Olle considered it really easy money: you carried a preppie on your back for a while, then he got knocked off by his opponent and ended up on his ass. It didn't even matter as long as the team itself won.

But he didn't have much information about the Black Knight—just some kid, according to him, with a black hood and a black mask who looked sort of mean. The Black Knight's horse was the crazy Mute, so it was no wonder no one could beat them.

"At first a lot of guys thought you were the Black Knight," Max was saying to Henning. "But I told them you weren't. You're much bigger than he is."

"Besides, the Mute doesn't live in our yard," said Henning.

According to the rules, horse and rider had to come from the same yard. And no one knew where the Black Knight lived—otherwise, it would have been easy to figure out who the Black Knight was.

"And then when you came to the tournament, everyone could see that you weren't the Black Knight," Max said almost sadly.

"Who's fighting the Karla Street Knights today?" said Henning. "Grand Street?"

Max nodded.

"I don't think it'll be much of a fight," Max said. "Karla Street's beaten nearly everybody."

"Of course. They have Christer," said Henning. He looked thoughtfully at me, as though he were mulling something over. But, "What time is it?" was all he said.

Max pulled out his pocket watch. It didn't seem to bother him at all that he looked ridiculous walking around with the kind of watch only old men would carry. He snapped the lid open and held it out accommodatingly.

"And then afterwards it'll be time for Nils-Wilhelm to fight the Black Knight from the Deepest Darkness. I wouldn't be surprised if Nils-Wilhelm doesn't have a pretty good chance against him."

"No way. The Black Knight is far superior in everything."

Henning got up. Stepping away from the oak tree, he looked like a legendary hero tearing himself loose from the trunk of a great tree, a hero who was just pausing there before setting out on a heroic quest. Oh, yes, if anyone could beat the Black Knight it was he; at that moment I was completely convinced.

Max looked at me. He was sensitive to moods, changes in feeling, and maybe he sensed my longing, for he said to Henning timidly, "Maybe Roland could come along?"

He turned to me with an explanation he really didn't need to make, "We're going over to the tournament to see the Black Knight."

Henning hesitated. I'd heard that only preppies were allowed in. Finally, he shrugged. "Sure. You can come."

"I don't have a cent," I said pitifully, almost ready to weep now that I finally had a chance to see the Black Knight. Money. Always the same problem. Even if the ticket didn't cost more than a few öre, I didn't have any money at all!

"You can borrow some from me," said Max.

Sometimes I borrowed money from him when I spent all my movie money; afterwards, I'd have an awful time paying it back. Max took out his famous black notebook and wrote down the loan.

"My father says the National Bank has lowered its interest rate," he grinned. "I better do the same thing or you'll run to the bank instead. Bankers have to be careful with their customers so that they'll keep bor-

12

rowing until they go bankrupt. Then the bank can take over the whole thing."

I'd seen the sign in the window of his father's firm in Harbor Street right next to Government Street and across the street from NK, the biggest department store in town: WENNERSTRAND'S BANKING HOUSE. Except for the fact that there were stocks and bonds in the window next to a lot of colorful foreign bills, it looked like an ordinary store.

"Maybe there won't be any tickets left," I said.

"People who come with Henning *always* get in," Max promised. "By the way, maybe we can get them to lower the price. Somebody said that Buffalo Bill is thinking of giving group tickets to people from the same yard."

I trotted along after them through the front portal of the building. Henning held the door open for me with a back as straight as a ruler—just the way the back of a son of a general in the Swedish Army should be.

3

The whole tournament had been Buffalo Bill's brainstorm.

The great organizer and showman of the neighborhood, he knew everybody and everybody knew him. As long as I could remember, it was he who'd organized all the shows, circuses, plays and contests in Ostermalm.

I especially remember the yo-yo contest. I'd considered entering, but the string of my yo-yo had broken and I didn't have money for a new one. But it was probably just as well; the preppies turned out to be real yo-yo sharks—for them, "Around the World" and "Walk the Dog" were just warm-up exercises.

Buffalo Bill was a preppie too. He was an open, friendly, pleasant type of kid, and he didn't seem to care whether you were a preppie or not. Even if he did charge admission and an entrance fee if you wanted to be in a contest, the first thing he wanted was to please, to entertain: he wanted everyone to have a good time.

His father had seen the real Buffalo Bill one day in May, 1905, in Paris, when Buffalo Bill had given a performance with his Wild West Show. At the time, the father had been a young man of 20, and he still considered the meeting (he had even shaken Buffalo Bill's hand) one of the biggest events in his life. For years afterwards he talked about that day in Paris as if he'd just gotten back; his most valuable possession was a poster for the show in French with Buffalo Bill's own signature on it.

When "our" Buffalo Bill turned eight, his father had given a big birthday party for him. One of his aunts asked him what he wanted to be when he grew up, and he answered calmly, "I'm gonna be like Buffalo Bill. I'm going to have my own circus."

Everybody laughed, but he just said it again: he was going to be a new Buffalo Bill. And so, ever since, he'd been called Buffalo Bill. Once when I told him that Buffalo Bill had been a real Indian scout, he looked at me with surprise: as far as he was concerned, Buffalo Bill had just been a ringmaster.

Once a year Buffalo Bill arranged a sort of world's fair where everyone could bring something to show. He called it "Strange and Wonderful Objects from All Four Corners of the World." You had to pay to look at the things, and the spectators would vote for the entry they thought was most interesting; the winner got a grand prize and also a quarter of the profits.

The last time he'd had the show I tried to find something at home to show, but we had absolutely nothing around.

"Well, we do have Catherine the Great's chamber pot," Poppa said. "That's pretty unusual, isn't it?"

But he was just kidding. We had two aunts named Catherine, but one was as big as a house, and that was why we called her Catherine the Great. But even if it had been the pot that the real Catherine the Great had peed in, it probably still wouldn't have won. The things that usually won were mechanical things—a battery-driven aerial circus, a ship sailing back and forth in a bottle, and, the year of the yo-yo contest, a little steam engine which ran a sort of mechanical picture: in it you could see a man smoking a pipe in a chair by the fireplace. When the man took his pipe from his mouth and blew the smoke out, the smoke went up the chimney. Everyone stared at it with fascination; they seemed to think that the old man might stop smoking or the fire might go out.

Sometimes I wondered if Buffalo Bill hadn't become a showman simply because he had such a fantastic yard. Surrounded by walls of neighboring houses on three sides, it looked at first as if it ended at a thick, chest-high wall about 10 or 12 meters from the fourth side, which was formed by a brick gable. But when you got closer you could see that this chest-high wall sliced the space in two, and to its right were steps which led down to another yard which was partially grass-covered and 3 or 4 meters below the big yard—a sort of sunken stage you could look down on from the top of the chest-high wall. In the walls on both sides of the lower yard there were doors, a tin door to the left and an ordinary wooden one to the right where the steps ended—this second one led to a hallway and then out to Maiden Street.

"The Black Knight comes in through that tin door," said Max. "It leads down to a cellar."

It was a perfect arena, hidden from curious eyes in the windows of the houses around the big yard. The spectators leaned over the top of the chest-high wall and looked down: the more daring ones sat astride the wall, and the most daring (Henning was the only one) sat and dangled his feet over the edge. The little kids who couldn't see above the wall at all could sit on the wooden staircase; they got in for half price. Buffalo Bill had his office under the staircase, and the ticket sales were in the big upper yard: a band of smaller boys was always at Buffalo Bill's beck and call.

Of course, Buffalo Bill had gotten the idea for the jousts from *Ivanhoe*. Everyone had either read the book or seen the movie at the matinee. Certain movies everyone had to see, just the way they had to read certain books which were passed around the neighborhood from hand to hand. *Son of the Rainbow* by Louis Tracy was one because it was so dirty, people said, with all that lovey-dovey stuff and everything;

The Condor by Øvre Richter-Frisch was another. Con*dom*, my sister would say. Mom, Roland's sitting with his *Condom* again! (She was a waitress in a place in a poor section way across town, and she had to get up at 4:30 every morning to get there.)

As we arrived, Buffalo Bill himself was selling tickets at a table made of a wooden plank and two sawhorses. His shiny moonface had a happy expression on it: one of his great assets was a phenomenal memory for names and faces, and as I came in he nodded at me.

"Hi, Roland! How's it going with your racing car? Prince Street is a little risky, but we could use Gärdet instead."

Henning and Max looked surprised. They hadn't known anything about my racing car. When Buffalo Bill shook hands with Henning, he asked him: "Aren't you going to challenge the Black Knight soon?"

Henning looked morose. It was a sensitive issue. Quickly Max leapt in: "Henning'll challenge the Black Knight when there's no one else left. Isn't that right, Henning?"

Henning nodded thoughtfully.

"Well," said Buffalo Bill, "Nils-Wilhelm's really the last one. The Black Knight is too tough for everyone else."

"How long will the tournament go on?" I asked.

"As long as there's a challenger. Or as long as the Black Knight wants to. He'll be a millionaire if this keeps on. Ten percent of the ticket sales! He sends the Mute to pick it up the day after."

"Is it true that you don't even know who he is?"

"Those are the rules. If someone wants to be anonymous, he can be," said Buffalo Bill, and he walked over to the wall.

About thirty spectators, all of them wearing school caps, were already leaning against it. The tallest rested their elbows on top of the wall. Everybody turned to greet Henning.

"Who do you like, Henning?"

"Do you think Karla Street will beat Grand?"

"Think Nils-Wilhelm has a chance against the Black Knight?"

To me they seemed a little too eager, as though they were trying to get on Henning's good side. He tossed off an answer:

"How can Karla Street lose? They've got Christer!"

As we approached the middle part of the wall, the preppies immediately made room for him; you could see how much they idolized him. Because I wasn't wearing a school cap, some of them weren't sure what to make of me.

"I think he goes to North Latin. Or to Beskow School," I heard someone say. I swelled with pride: they thought I was a preppie!

The stairs to the right were already completely filled; little kids peered delightedly through the railing out over the arena. From the edge of the wall where we stood it was, as I said, about 3 or 4 meters to the ground. Henning swung himself easily up on the edge, and there he sat dangling his legs over what we considered an abyss. One or two of the other preppies copied him but quickly retreated—it made you all queasy in the stomach—to safer positions with their elbows leaning against the top of the wall.

"If you fell down, you'd break a leg at the very least."

"Not Henning. You should see him on the wooden horses in gym class. He's incredible. Really incredible!"

Graffiti was scrawled in all different colors of chalk on the rough brick opposite us.

"Down with the Bolsheviks!" someone had written all over. "P Loves T." "Who's On First, What's On Second, And I Don't Know His Name's On Third!" All kinds of nonsense like that. But next to the wall was a sugar crate painted yellow and blue, the Swedish national colors. It was set on end, and on it sat a real Boy Scout in his uniform and a red scarf, munching on an apple.

A Scout—that was something I longed to be with all my heart. A kid named Nick in our class had told us about Scouting and camping and all the merit badges you could get.

"Tell your mother and father—they can sign you up. You have to start out as a Cub Scout."

But my parents didn't want me to be a Scout.

"It's just for rich kids," said Poppa at first. When I continued to nag him about it, I realized that he

20

thought there was something peculiar about the Scouts—or at least about their leaders.

"They have pansies for leaders. Not real men. Do you want to be in the Asshole Patrol?"

In front of the space under the stairs where Buffalo Bill usually had his office hung a white curtain which looked suspiciously like a regular white sheet. Now and then a head stuck out and peered up towards the spectators.

"That's Yngve from Karla Street! And that's Ossian from Grand," said the all-knowing Max.

"The knights change in there," he continued. "And over there is where the horses wait."

I leaned out over the edge and looked to the left. Close to the tin door was an enclosure bordered by wooden sawhorses, the kind they use in roadwork. About ten boys were in the enclosure; Olle was leaning on a sawhorse with some other boys I recognized from classes parallel to mine in school. Sixten, another classmate, crouched on the ground playing Territory, a knife game.

I pulled my head back quickly; I didn't want to be seen. It felt wonderful to be a preppie, and I wanted to enjoy every second of it.

The preppies were talking about the coming events—Karla vs. Grand Street, Nils-Wilhelm vs. the Black Knight. They kept asking Henning, "So what do you *really* think? Does Nils-Wilhelm have a chance?"

Finally Henning shook his head in annoyance.

Max was standing next to him, holding a corner of his jacket as though he were afraid of Henning falling off.

"Nils-Wilhelm doesn't have quick enough reflexes," Henning said.

Immediately they all agreed. Of course. Nils-Wilhelm doesn't have quick enough reflexes. It was so simple. Just like when he lets the ball roll through his legs in soccer, even when it's slow!

Amused, Max noted the effect of Henning's royal words. He bragged, "Everybody knows that Henning's the only one who can beat the Black Knight!"

Suddenly the clear voice of a girl rang out behind us.

"Here comes the Black Knight! Get up and fight, Henning! I'm going to sweep the field up with you!"

Everyone turned around.

"Rebecca!" said Max.

She stood a few steps away. Her dark brown eyes twinkled with pleasure; she loved getting everyone's attention. She'd picked up a long brush from one of the buckets in the corner of the yard, and she was pointing it towards us like a lance.

"Rebecca!" said all the preppies.

4

Who knows? Buffalo Bill may have started the tournament just because we, like Ivanhoe, had our own special Rebecca.

Rebecca was Max's cousin, and she turned up every now and then in our yard. Like Henning, she was best at everything in her school, said Max, but the strange thing was (according to Max again) that the same things which made Henning the unquestioned leader of the boy preppies made the girls avoid Rebecca. Actually, I thought they were just envious. Not because she was the best at everything, but because she was so beautiful. She had dark hair, brown, sunny eyes, and long legs which carried her in a soft, supple way—a way unlike that of any other girl I'd ever seen. She was both beautiful and spirited—and maybe it was her spirit I fell for most.

One time when she'd sat behind me in the movies, I was so aware of her presence, of her quiet chatter to a girlfriend and her clear laughter, that the movie became a total jumble for me. And whenever she came to our yard, she had only to give me a nod to make me feel like one of the Chosen. For days afterwards I'd live off that nod, the sunny gleam in her eye and her sudden laugh.

Mom caught on quickly to things. She was hanging out wash in the yard one day where lines were stretched between two houses.

"Who was that girl?" she said.

"Max's cousin."

"I could tell they were related."

"But they don't look alike."

"No, but you can see that she has Jewish blood. It's strange that she's got a crush on the general's boy. Usually the Jews stick to their own."

A crush on Henning! I didn't believe it! Wasn't she always arguing and fighting with him from the moment she arrived? And didn't he seem completely indifferent to her, almost snubbing her—which didn't seem to worry her at all?

Take now, for instance. He turned halfway around and looked irritatedly at her and the broad brush, and he shook his head disdainfully. Buffalo Bill came running over with a determined expression on his round face; he didn't want her to make fun of the tournament's main attraction and distract the spectators.

"If you're going to stay, you have to buy a ticket!"

That was the first thing he always thought about.

Rebecca swung the brush over towards him. You could tell how much she loved being the center of attention. When she came in, everybody's back had been turned to her; now, in one second, they'd all turned around. Everyone, that is, except Henning. He turned his back to her again.

"Why do *I* have to buy a ticket? Can't you see that I'm the Black Knight? Don't you see my lance? I ought to *get* paid instead. Doesn't anyone want to fight?"

"Don't make a fool of yourself!" yelled Max.

"Let her go on," said Henning over his shoulder. "She can be the court jester."

She danced back and forth while Max and Buffalo Bill tried to get the brush away from her. She poked them playfully in the ribs; some of the preppies laughed and others applauded and called: "Go get him, Black Knight!"

"Come on, Henning, you chicken! Get up and fight the Black Knight!"

"He's got to get a horse first," protested Max.

"What's wrong with Roland? He can be the horse."

She pointed the brush at me. Buffalo Bill quickly grabbed it, and I turned red as a beet. My legs almost crumpled beneath me; it was the first time she'd ever said my name.

But at the same time what she said had made it very clear that I belonged with the horses, that I was a public school kid who didn't have any business among the rich kids. Suddenly I regretted bitterly

25

that I came along with Henning and Max. I thought that everyone was staring at me and thinking, "What are you doing here, you poor man's kid?" And suddenly I became aware of the holes in my socks (even though you couldn't see them through my worn sneakers), my unwashed shirt, my frayed and spotted pants, my long hair—and the musty smell of poverty all over me.

"Henning's too heavy for him," Max answered.

"I don't think Henning has the *guts* to challenge the Black Knight!"

Rebecca had a special way of emphasizing certain words. The way she said *guts* wasn't exactly scornful, just challenging in a taunting way, and with a little laugh in it too. Exactly like her *"I"* earlier: "Do *I* have to buy a ticket?" It had sounded comical, as if the thought itself was absurd.

While the others rushed to defend Henning—of *course* he had the guts!—Henning himself turned around.

"Don't worry. I'll fight him. And then you can bring your broom and sweep up what's left of him!"

"You have to buy a *ticket,*" groaned Buffalo Bill. "We're just about to start."

"I didn't come here to waste my time watching your tournament. I came to borrow some money from my cousin *Max.*"

The last word was said in such a demanding tone that Max immediately pulled out his black notebook and walked to the other side of the yard with her.

Buffalo Bill sent one of his helpers off to the wash buckets with the brush, saying, "Keep an eye on her. Make sure she really leaves. We don't want *any* gate-crashers!"

I was glad the attention had turned towards the arena again. But I felt uncomfortable and outside of things, and I knew now that everyone knew who I was—I'd never stand here among the preppies again. Max returned.

"That Rebecca! She's just impossible! But as long as she pays back her loans with interest, I can't complain!"

I turned around.

She was on her way out, her back as straight as Henning's. In the doorway she turned towards us; she stretched both arms in front of her, made a fist of her left hand and then slowly pulled back her right arm (also with a fisted hand) as though she were drawing a bow. She aimed straight at us. Then her right arm jerked back and her hand stretched out as though the arrow had left the bow—the whole thing was very realistic.

"Now she's playing Robin Hood," Max said. "The great archer. She should be going to an acting school instead of New Elementary for Girls."

Suddenly I started. From the arena below sounded a bugle blast which echoed between the walls of the houses and pierced me to the marrow.

5

A real live bugler!

I could hardly believe my ears or my eyes. The bugler was the apple-eating Boy Scout. I hadn't noticed his bugle before. Now he was standing on the yellow and blue sugar crate by the brick wall, and a blue and yellow pennant fluttered from the bugle in his hand. In his blue uniform and red scarf, he looked like a real herald. He wasn't very big, but could he ever blow that horn!

The festive fanfare threw us suddenly into the world of *Ivanhoe*. The brick wall behind the herald darkened, became obscure, and out of it grew an almost impenetrable oak forest. The gables of the houses at either end of the yard turned into pointed palisades, and we, we became a brilliant retinue of noblemen—dukes, barons and earls. The vivid notes went straight to our hearts, filling us with courage and bravery—all because of that jubilant bugle fanfare. The heroes of tournaments and battles in times gone by talked directly to us, spurred us on, urged us to accomplish great deeds.

All my nervousness vanished.

I knew it was the sound of the bugle that did it. We almost never heard live music, and we were always thirsting for it. Music opened our senses, overwhelmed us, gave our world color and made us quiver with excitement and joy—and brought tears of happiness to our eyes. We'd run to Grand Street the minute we heard the Salvation Army Band! They played and sang so well we all felt like joining up on the spot. And when we saw the King's Guard parading through the streets—well, we'd even forget to go to the Sunday matinees. And the street musicians— why didn't millions of kronor pour down on them when they sang and played and everybody rushed to the window to listen, enjoy, applaud?

When the last note had died away, a group of knights stepped out from the room under the stairs. I stared at them, struck dumb with amazement. It was like magic. They had gone in as preppies, but now they were knights. Everyone had helmets on, and tunics in green or blue. The knights in green wore a straight white collar slit at the shoulders; the blue knights wore yellow collars. When you looked down at them—as we did—from above, the helmets and collars dominated, white and yellow, and it was a sunny, happy sight. In their hands they held long, pointed lances.

Buffalo Bill made his way down the steps through the crowd of little kids. As usual, he was wearing his black cape. He loved to unfurl it with a grand gesture—"Let the show begin!"—and he stood in the middle of the arena and welcomed everyone. Then he made a sweeping gesture up towards the top of the wall which he ended dramatically by pointing towards the horses in the enclosure. In an unusually rich and resonant voice he declared:

"*Largesse, largesse,* ladies and gentlemen!"

The middle of the wall where we were standing suddenly became empty as everyone rushed off to the left, above the horses' enclosure. Down there my schoolmates crowded together, their upturned faces a bunch of pale spots except for one or two brown faces—poor wretches who had been forced to go to the school's summer camp.

"*Largesse, largesse,* honorable gentlemen and beautiful ladies!"

The audience crowded together by the wall. They started throwing money, copper and silver coins, down to the horses. It was like throwing meat to starving wolves: arms and legs whirled in the air, heads banged together, large clumps of earth went flying. Their yells and shouts were shrill, angry, and urgent. "I saw it first!" "Hey, what're you doing?" "That's mine!" Some crawled around on all fours, searching for coins. Others tried to catch the money in mid-air. I saw the usually quiet Olle throw himself after a coin, pushing Sixten away so that he fell flat on his back. Now and then someone actually caught a coin in the air, and then the preppies applauded. But mostly they pointed and laughed delightedly.

"Look at the guy in the brown shirt! He really got clouted! Throw towards the left! They're fighting like mad over there!"

I couldn't join in their pleasure. I was envious. I wanted to be down there instead. I'd have made sure to get some of those coins! And I was surprised that Olle hadn't said a word about the preppies' throwing money to the horses; it seemed as though he'd wanted to keep it a secret. But maybe he was just afraid that I'd become a horse too, and then there would be one more person to compete with.

Money was something we didn't have very much of. We'd have to do a lot of nagging (and then not always successfully) just to get money for the Sunday matinee. At around 11:00 we'd start making the rounds of the movie theaters in Ostermalm—from the Sibyll behind the National Theater to the Paris on Roslags Street. *Arizona Bound* with Gary Cooper, *Parade of the West* with Ken Maynard, *The Mounted Stranger*—what arguments we'd have, what agonies about which one to see!

And there was so much we wanted. Big things, little things. Tin soldiers from Gemla on Master Samuel Street, soccer balls, compasses, Texas Jack novels, Erector sets. I thought of following in the footsteps of Jonas Fjeld and becoming a master criminal just so that I could afford my great dream, the "O" model

Erector set. And since we didn't have any money, all the things the preppies owned became objects of longing. Money was like a river that seemed to gush for a few rich people, then ran further to a whole group of slightly less rich people—storekeepers and craftsmen—and by the time it got to our dads, the workers and unskilled laborers down at the bottom, it shrank to a miserable trickle. Our outstretched hands never got filled with any money at all—not a red cent.

"Look, two of them are still fighting," said Max, "even though the money stopped."

Henning had been sitting swinging his legs on the edge of the wall; now he cast a casual look to the side.

"It's good for them to get mad at each other. Makes them better horses. Toughens them up."

The preppies took their places again along the wall. My horse friends got up and wiped off the grass and earth. Each one stood alone: those who'd done best counted up the loot with quick, watchful glances in all directions, as though they were afraid that some of the others would try to take it away. Then, with a pleased grin, they'd stuff the money into their pants pockets, followed by the sullen, envious eyes of the others. No one said a word.

"And now, honorable gentlemen and beautiful ladies, it's time for the grand battle between the Karla Street Knights and the Knights of Grand Street," announced Buffalo Bill.

32

He read the rules out loud; they were simple and easy to understand. The tournament was open only to "knights of noble lineage" (that is to say, preppies) who rode horses from their own yards. A rider who touched both feet to the ground would be considered eliminated. A knight who was forced by his opponent back against the wall was also eliminated, as was a horse who was forced to his knees. And a knight who hit his opponent's horse with his lance was automatically disqualified.

Then, for the first time, I noticed a pile of cork, cone-shaped contraptions next to the blue and yellow box. The sharp points of the lances were to be wedged into them to dull the impact.

"Otherwise, they could go right through someone," said Max. "Those lances are really sharp!"

At Buffalo Bill's signal the horses lumbered over to the box and formed a double line, five guys in each column, just like we did in the schoolyard before we marched into the classroom. The knights gathered on Buffalo Bill's other side, ten of them just like the horses. The bugler stood behind the box, rubbing the bugle on his sleeve.

"Karla Street is good," said Max. "They're like the Musketeers—one for all and all for one."

"How's Grand Street?" I asked.

"Individuals. They don't have the kind of leader Karla Street has in Christer. He's really good. He fires them all up."

The knights on both sides started to get ready. The

horse would stand still, and the knight would climb on his back with his feet on either side of the horse's body. They had to make sure that the knight's knees were locked in securely by the horse's arms so that the knight had a firm seat—some of the horses locked their hands together across their chests while others put their thumbs in their belts, all so that they wouldn't suddenly lose their grip and let their riders slide off.

Before he returned the lances to the knights, Buffalo Bill made sure that all the pieces of cork were properly fastened to the lance tips.

"Take your places," he finally said.

The two groups of knights and horses went to their respective sides, the Karla Street Knights in green, the Grand Street Knights in blue. Some of my friends carried their riders in a completely relaxed way, as though they had no burden at all on their backs. Others looked like they were straining: they clenched their teeth and stared in concentration in front of them. The knights tried to find the best positions for their lances.

On Olle's broad back was a rather solid-looking preppie who looked content and happy as he lifted his lance point towards us. Around us everyone was cheering. Most people rooted for Grand Street; Karla Street wasn't in our neighborhood, and everyone thought that the Karla Street Knights were braggarts.

Finally they all stood ready on opposite sides of the yard. Christer, the leader of the Karla Street Knights, was a slender, lithe boy with a green pennant on his lance shaft. He looked quite self-confident as he raised his lance and cried:

"For King and Country!"

He lifted it higher. All his comrades shouted in unison:

"For King and Country!"

Buffalo Bill shaped his hands into a funnel and shouted:

"Laissez aller!"

A short blast of the bugle drowned out all other noise—and the two lines started moving towards each other.

6

Each team's fans were sitting in separate groups, and they tried to outshout each other with group cheers just as if they were at a soccer match between Sweden and Denmark.

Go, go Karla Knights!
Show them you can really fight!

Down in the arena the green and blue lines rushed full speed at each other. Olle ran like a madman, and Sixten was only a few steps behind to his right—Sixten who always got hit when we played "Monkey in the Middle" because he was so slow! Some of the knights crouched low on their horses' bent backs so that they would make smaller targets, while others sat more upright. Olle looked resolute and full of energy; he really wanted the extra money he'd get if his side won.

Since Olle and Sixten were the right flank of the Grand Street Knights, neither of them had to go up against Christer. I recognized Christer's horse; he'd played center on a soccer team that had played our class in Ostermalm Sports Park at a tournament for all the public schools.

When the teams were 7 or 8 meters from each other, Grand Street raised their lances—each one expected to take on an opponent in front of him. But suddenly Christer shouted:

"Switch!"

The knights on both his flanks quickly changed places. Confused, the Grand Street Knights lowered their lances, not sure of what to do. Nothing more was needed. One of the Karla Street Knights moved out front and jabbed his lance against the shoulder of his hesitant opponent. The legs of the Grand Street Knight flew up, and his lance flew out of his hand in an arc behind him. He couldn't regain his balance, and he fell to the ground with a dull thud, his helmet rattling beside him.

There was a shout of triumph from one of the Karla Street fans.

Karla's Green wins the fray;
We'll beat the Blue Team any day!

At the same time Olle's knight managed to hit his opponent's side squarely. The Karla Street knight shrieked, dropped his lance, and groped wildly in the air until he fell backwards. It looked horrible, but he managed to turn at just the last moment so that he hit the ground on his side. Now the Grand Street fans shouted.

We'll bring the Green down to defeat—
Like grass we'll trample them under our feet!

Christer held himself somewhat behind his team, keeping his opponent at a distance with short parries from his penannt-bedecked lance. He directed his knights in a sharp, high voice, "Go ahead, Ossian! Circle him, Sven!"

Confused by his orders, the horses of the Grand Street team didn't know what to do. Sixten backed up but took a false step; he and his rider tripped and fell over each other on the ground and a shout of delight went up from the Karla Street side. Christer feigned a thrust, his opponent's lance flew up to parry it, and Christer knocked the lance to the side; the blow knocked the Grand Street boy off balance, and he slid down his horse's back.

Now there were only two Grand Street Knights left. They moved closer to each other and stood, side by side, ready to fend off the four Karla Street Knights as best they could. Sand and gravel whirled all over as the six of them trampled around the arena. A ray of sun found its way down through a space between the massive buildings around us—or was it a reflection from a high window? Long shadows danced on the brick wall in a lively, curious ballet.

Olle's shirt was soaked—sweat ran off him, and he was constantly adjusting his grip on his rider's legs. The fight grew more heated. Olle pushed and shoved the enemy horses with lowered head, trying to make them lose their balance and their grip on the riders' legs. But nothing worked; there were too many of them. He and his friend, the other Grand Street horse, were driven back. Finally one of the Karla Street Knights managed to get a jab of his lance in the belly of the knight next to Olle. He fell to the side, grabbed Olle's knight and dragged him down with him. A disappointed "Nooo!" went up from the top of the wall.

The Karla Street Knights pointed their lances in the air, and their fans hooted:

Karla Street has won the day!
They beat Grand Street—that's the way!

Exhausted, the horses massed in front of the water faucet sticking out from the wall next to the cellar door. They stood nervously fidgeting, and then stuck their heads under the faucet and drank, letting the water pour over their heads. The knights went in under the stairs to take off their costumes and collars, and Buffalo Bill stepped forward and announced an intermission before the great battle between Nils-Wilhelm and the Black Knight.

I was surprised by the violence of the whole spectacle—by no means had it been a harmless business. One knight had a bloody nose; he went inside, holding his head tilted backwards. A second knight limped, a third rubbed his side and grimaced. The horses all looked like they'd come out okay.

During the whole battle I'd stood at an angle behind Henning, who had watched in silence. But no sooner had Buffalo Bill collected the cork cones than I was pushed aside by eager preppies. "Henning, what did you think? It was just like you said! Karla Street was just too good, right?"

"Why do you think they lost?" someone said.

He didn't answer immediately. First he raised a hand in greeting to Christer down in the arena—Christer was the last to go behind the curtain by the stairs. Finally he said, "Grand Street's attack was too weak."

Everyone nodded sagely. Of course, Grand Street's attack was much too weak. But what about Christer's presence of mind, his leadership, the way he'd outmaneuvered his opponents?

I was sure Henning was wrong, that it was Christer who'd given Karla Street the advantage . . . and I tried to work my way towards saying it by asking Max timidly, "This guy Nils-Wilhelm who's going to fight the Black Knight—is he as good as Christer?"

Max stared wide-eyed at me and answered in amazement, "Are you joking? Nils-Wilhelm is a Prince Magnus Street Knight!"

Some of the preppies were tugging at Max's arm; they wanted to bet on the fight, and Max was the

40

official bookie. As they milled around in the arena, Buffalo Bill's helpers walked among the preppies selling tickets to the "American Lottery" in which the winner would get a xylophone. They kept the tickets in paper bags, and some of the preppies were lucky enough to get tickets with low numbers. Since the number on the ticket was also its price, they could afford to buy several. I was dying to get one too, but I didn't have an öre left; Max's loan had just paid for the price of admission.

Buffalo Bill was talking with everybody. He was trying to set up a new team to go against the losing Grand Street team. They didn't have to come from a particular block or neighborhood, and anyone could be on the team.

"We'll call them the Nameless Knights," he said.

But nobody seemed to be very interested—he spoke to everybody but me, but of course I wasn't "of noble birth."

By the carpet rack they'd actually set up a bar. There was a long line in front of it because someone had said that Buffalo Bill had spiked the sodas with rum that he'd stolen from home.

"Captain Morgan's rum! Genuine pirate rum!"

Suddenly we heard a girl's indignant voice. Rebecca stood in the middle of the yard surrounded by preppies, a worried lottery ticket seller in front of her. Buffalo Bill rushed towards them, his cape flapping behind him. Rebecca pointed accusingly at the ticket seller:

"I *won't* pay the 90 öre! I didn't get to choose the

ticket myself. And I think he *knew* it was a ticket with a high number!"

She spoke clearly and distinctly with that special way of hers of emphasizing certain words, but you had the feeling that the anger was just on the surface. An amused glint in her brown eyes and an almost imperceptible smile at the corners of her mouth took the sting out of her words. You got the feeling that she wasn't really mad; she just liked making a fuss so that she'd be the center of attention again.

"I thought you'd gone," said Buffalo Bill.

"I'm not going to disturb your little tournament. I'll leave as soon as I get a ticket, a ticket with a low number."

Buffalo Bill protested. How would it look if everyone under the sun came and said that he wanted to change his ticket just because he'd gotten a high number? You had to take your chances—that was the whole point of an American lottery.

"You *have* to pay!"

"Never! And anyway—where's the xylophone? Maybe it isn't even worth ten öre!"

Henning appeared outside the circle of preppies—he just pushed a little and those who· stood closest made room immediately when they saw who it was. He seemed to take control as though he realized that he was the only one who could handle Rebecca.

"When you buy a ticket, you take your chances."

"I'm willing to pay if it's an honest game. But when they try to pawn a high number off on me . . ."

"Give me a ticket!" Henning commanded.

42

The ticket seller shuffled through the tickets, shut his eyes and selected one at random; he put it in Henning's outstretched hand. Henning rolled the brown ticket open and showed it to Rebecca and everybody else.

"Ninety-five!" echoed the voices. "That's the worst!"

Calmly, Henning took a handful of change from his jacket pocket and counted out 95 öre. The ticket seller put the money in his cigar box and wrote Henning's name after the number 95 on his list. A low mumbling rose from the crowd.

"Henning really is a good sport! He doesn't complain even when he loses!"

"He's a cool guy, that's for sure!"

But Rebecca objected, "He certainly didn't close his eyes when he picked *my* ticket!"

"That's not so strange. Who'd want to close his eyes with you in front of him?" Henning asked.

The preppies smiled broadly and nudged each other. Rebecca met Henning's steady gaze and thoughtfully bit her lower lip.

"What exactly is that supposed to mean?"

"Take it any way you like."

They stood opposite each other, he blond, she dark, both straight-backed, proud and self-assured. Mom's words came back to me, "Rebecca's got a crush on the general's kid." I shrank, I froze, I felt like I was shivering at the outer circle of a campfire that gave off warmth and sparks.

"Ninety-five! You always have to be the worst!"

Rebecca paid for her ticket and went out through the yard door, but then turned and shouted, "But I'm certainly going to be at the drawing just to make sure everything's on the up and up. Don't think you can cheat me just because I'm not a boy and I don't go to Ostra Prep!"

The door slammed after her.

"I just took the first one I saw and gave it to her," the ticket seller moaned. Buffalo Bill put his hand on the kid's head and roughed up his hair in a friendly way. "Don't worry about it. You know how girls are. Try to get rid of the rest of the tickets, and we'll start the tournament again."

He escorted Henning back to the wall and spoke eagerly about his plans for the future.

"Dart throwing and fishing poles with magnets. What do you think? A big fall festival. But *no* American lottery!"

7

Finally I was going to see the Black Knight!

Except for the bugler standing by the blue and yellow crate near the wall, the arena was completely deserted. Some of my horse-buddies hadn't left yet, and Buffalo Bill let them sit for free on the ground below the stairs. Up where I was, the preppies pushed and jostled each other to get a better view, but they were quieter, more expectant, than they had been before the battle between Karla and Grand Streets. They kept looking towards the cellar door to the left, the door through which the Black Knight would come.

Behind the locked tin door there was a cellar with long, winding passages that disappeared into the Unknown. No preppies had ever explored the place completely, and people said there were actually *two* levels of the cellar, that underneath the first was another from the Middle Ages. Sometimes, they said, you could find connecting passages between the two:

a damp, dripping staircase or a cramped, nearly caved-in tunnel. If you went down into those catacombs, you might get totally lost.

"They've even found human bones down there," said Christer. An even-tempered, talkative boy who stood proudly right next to Henning; he'd already changed back into his street clothes and school cap.

"Yeah, down in the old cellar," said Henning.

"And they say that it runs under a lot of different sections of town. So people probably *do* get lost down there if they don't have flashlights and they have to find their way around in the dark."

"The Black Knight probably doesn't have any trouble down there," said Max. "He and the Devil come from the same place."

"So far we haven't seen his tail or his hooves," said Henning drily.

The Black Knight would appear out of that darkness which we'd created in our heads and which was filled with secret, frightening powers. And maybe that was what attracted and disturbed us most: he seemed to personify the dark powers in ourselves that we didn't really want to admit to, and which we were just as unwilling to explore as the real, winding passages in the cellar.

Buffalo Bill put a cork cone next to the doors on either end of the arena. The Boy Scout bugler got up on his box and wiped off the mouthpiece of his brass bugle. Buffalo Bill chatted a moment with the little kids who were packed together like sardines on the thirteen steps of the staircase. They giggled; he looked at the clock. The audience whistled; they were as eager as if they were at a movie matinee and the lights had just been turned off.

Finally Buffalo Bill went to the middle of the arena and raised his arm. The soft murmuring diminished, the whistles stopped. In his black cape he looked like a magician, like Dante the Magnificent who packed the circus to the rafters every week—but whom I'd only seen on posters.

"Honorable gentlemen and beautiful ladies!" said Buffalo Bill. (That was one of his favorite expressions for all kinds of occasions, not just during the tournament.) "You are about to see the great battle between the challenger, the Knight of Prince Magnus Street, and the as yet undefeated Black Knight, the Black Knight from the Deepest Darkness!"

He took sure, decisive strides towards the wooden door to the right. Then he turned around and looked out over the arena to make sure everything was ready. Someone yelled impatiently: "Open it, for crissakes!"

At that moment the Scout put the bugle to his lips. A noisy (but to my ears far too brief) fanfare sounded, and Buffalo Bill threw open the door.

In came the most perfect Knight of Brightness imaginable!

"Jesus, will you look at that!"

"Nils-Wilhelm got himself a completely new costume!"

"He looks like Richard the Lionhearted himself!"

Nils-Wilhelm was dressed in a brilliantly shining battle tunic, a silvery-looking helmet and a silver collar fringed with silver, triangular-shaped trimming and covered with silver stars. Even his lance was covered with silver-white paint. He was broad-shouldered, and he had an energetically jutting chin and a determined expression on his face. He sat on the back of a well-built boy whom I had seen a few times in the schoolyard; I didn't know which class he was in, though—our school was pretty big.

The gleaming knight and his sturdy horse exuded self-confidence and strength; they were of a completely different caliber from the Karla and Grand Street Knights. Nils-Wilhelm lowered the sharp tip of his lance toward Buffalo Bill who put the cork cone on carefully. The audience had been cheering all this time, and now they began to shout.

"Hey, Nils-Wilhelm, give the Black Knight what he's been asking for!"

"Tear off his mask!"

"Naw, tear off his head!"

Nils-Wilhelm laughed, grinned at the crowd for a moment, then fished out a sugar cube and put it in his horse's mouth. The horse bent his head several times, smacked his lips and scraped his boot against the ground—and then cantered around the arena. The crowd loved it.

"Clowning," said Henning. He did not approve.

In the meantime Buffalo Bill had walked over to

the tin door at the opposite side of the arena. Ceremoniously he pulled out a large key which he put in the keyhole and turned as though he were unlocking the cage of a fierce wild animal. The bugle sounded again, short and warlike. Buffalo Bill flung the door open. The noise and commotion stopped, and everyone became completely silent.

The Black Knight entered the arena.

The Black Knight!

Yes, he was truly black, the blackest thing I'd ever seen. He had no helmet, only a black hood which fell far down over his shoulders. His face was covered by a black cloth which had narrow slits for eyes and almost unnoticeable holes for his nose and mouth. His battle tunic was black, his pants were black, his boots were black. At first I thought his hands were black too, but then I noticed that he was wearing gloves; that seemed to me very sophisticated. Like Nils-Wilhelm, he'd painted his lance—only black of course, except for the metal tip which glittered menacingly.

"The Black Knight!" someone said loudly and completely gratuitously. But no one laughed. The sun had disappeared; so had the light reflections which had played over the arena earlier. The day grew pale, shrivelled and gray, as though the Black Knight had frightened the light away.

He wasn't tall or powerfully built, but he carried himself incredibly erect, almost in a military way. He sat absolutely still, only turning his head to look up at us and then at the waiting Nils-Wilhelm. Even though I hadn't seen him in action yet, I knew for sure that he'd be as quick and subtle as a reptile.

He lowered his lance, and Buffalo Bill fastened the cone to the sharp metal tip. The horse stood as unmoving as a statue; only the eyes moved, and *they* looked in every direction. As usual, the Mute was on his guard!

He was a broad boy with muscular arms and a wide face; his black hair made him look almost foreign. No one knew his name or where he lived; he moved all over Ostermalm. Of course, he was supposed to live in the same yard as the Black Knight, but no one knew where *he* lived either.

Olle's theory was that the Mute was probably some kind of vampire. "He sleeps in graveyards at night and sucks blood to give him strength during the day."

"And what about the Black Knight?"

"Oh, he's from the same yard—the graveyard, ha ha! He's a corpse or a ghost."

In any case, the Mute did seem to have slept in his clothes. They were torn and tattered, and his blue sneakers were completely frayed. He couldn't speak, just pant and snort. It sounded horrible. He frightened us, for there was an intensity about him which was really scary. Fiercely, he stared straight ahead, and in that look was wildness, madness, and something else, something even stranger which made us feel helpless and stupid, as though what he was saying with his eyes was something we couldn't understand at 'all. Even the grown-ups were afraid of him. At the market place they threw fruit and vegetables just to get rid of him.

"Here you go! Now beat it!"

But the fact that the Black Knight had tamed the Mute was in itself something of a miracle. What mysterious powers did he have to make the Mute—so unbending and independent—into a two-legged horse?

Buffalo Bill stepped back to the Scout. No one shouted anything to Nils-Wilhelm; no one shouted at all. The silence was almost creepy. What a difference from when the Karla and Grand Street Knights were fighting! Was it the Black Knight's mask that made the preppies so nervous? What was he hiding behind it? A disfigured face? Maybe no face at all—just a skull? There were plenty of theories, but most of the preppies suspected that he was one of their mortal enemies, a kid from North Latin.

Max insisted that it could be one of their own—Hakon, for example. Henning dismissed it. "Hakon has glasses. He's nearsighted."

And the Black Knight did not have glasses.

"Maybe Carl Magnus. He has tonsilitis, and he's so hoarse he can't even speak." (The Black Knight was just as silent as the Mute.) "But Carl Magnus," said Christer, "still has a fever and can't get out of bed."

The two knights stood ready, one black, the other shimmering like a Knight of the Sun. Buffalo Bill raised his hands again in the shape of a funnel and shouted.

"Laissez aller!"

The bugle sounded. The two started moving towards each other, and at the same time a roar rose up from the preppies, a roar so loud that it almost burst my eardrums.

The Mute was incredibly fast. He got to the middle of the arena a full ten meters ahead of Nils-Wilhelm. The two knights lowered their lances at each other. The trick was to hit the other at such high speed and with such momentum that your opponent would be knocked right off his horse.

The Black Knight and the Mute were like a single person. The Knight maneuvered him with his knees and sat so securely on his back that he could hold the lance with both hands. He thrust at Nils-Wilhelm. Nils-Wilhelm tried to parry, but at the last moment the Black Knight pulled back his lance and the Mute made a quick, unexpectedly graceful leap to one side. Nils-Wilhelm had force behind the parry, but neither his opponent nor his lance was there to receive it, and he almost fell off his horse. A startled "Ah!" went through the crowd.

They passed each other. Quick as lightning the Mute turned around. Nils-Wilhelm had to wait for a while before his clumsy horse figured out what was going on ("Turn around, idiot!") and could pivot totally around. When he finally did, Nils-Wilhelm saw that the Mute was right up against him.

He thrust his lance out desperately, but the Mute just glided by him, and the Black Knight avoided the blow. It looked absolutely death-defying: the Black Knight was hanging far out on the side of the Mute's back. With incredible speed, the Mute circled Nils-Wilhelm, and before anyone had time to understand what had happened he was on the other side of his adversary.

After his unsuccessful thrust, Nils-Wilhelm was still off-balance. The Black Knight hit, no, nudged him with the lance; the wide cone caught him in the side. Flailing his arms and legs Nils-Wilhelm screamed, and, fencing with his arms, he fell to the ground, pulling his horse down with him.

A cry of anger, disappointment, and booing came from the crowd, mixed with desperate encouragement.

"Get up and fight, Nils-Wilhelm!"

But everyone knew that the fight was over. The Black Knight had won again.

8

It was the most fantastic thing I'd ever seen.

And just as fantastic was the overpowering, almost sensual feeling of happiness which flowed through me and made me forget myself and everything around me. It was a feeling I didn't want to give up; I just wanted to get deeper and deeper into it. With all my heart I wished that Nils-Wilhelm would follow their advice and get up so that I could see the Black Knight outmaneuver him again.

It was as if they'd defied the law of gravity; I couldn't remember one time that the Mute's sneakers had touched the ground. The Black Knight and the Mute had floated over the ground—quickly, lightly, elegantly—and their effortless precision had made Nils-Wilhelm and his horse look like prehistoric monsters.

Now I knew why the tournament was such a big success, why the preppies came in droves and were willing to pay a high entrance fee. Who wouldn't pay to be part of a such a spectacle? I'd half-believed that Nils-Wilhelm's weight could literally crush the lighter Black Knight, but Nils-Wilhelm hadn't had a chance. Of course the preppies wanted the Black Knight to be defeated and unmasked. But I knew they also wanted—with a mixture of fear and delight—for him to continue his streak of victories and become a myth, a hero who was so great that they'd be proud even to have seen him once in their lives.

The preppies were still booing Nils-Wilhelm who plodded, limping slightly, back to the stairs with his lance dragging behind him—he wasn't shining so brightly anymore. His horse was still on all fours, hammering his fist against the ground and swearing a long string of curses.

"What did I say? His reflexes weren't quick enough."

Henning sounded more bitter than triumphant. For once he hadn't sat on the edge nonchalantly swinging his legs; he'd stood up with the rest of us leaning against the wall. Once, during the final stage of the joust, he'd let out a half-smothered cry, "No, no, Nils-Wilhelm, not like *that!*"

"Who do you think's going to beat the Black Knight when not even Nils-Wilhelm can do it?" asked Christer.

It grew completely quiet around Henning.

Nobody needed to say a word. Everybody was thinking the same thing that Rebecca had said, "You

chicken, you don't have the guts to challenge him!"
For she had a way of putting into words what many
of the preppies couldn't say out loud—at least so that
Henning could hear it. Who was better qualified to
take on the Black Knight than Henning—the best
track and field preppie in the city, and a fencer that
even the older kids had trouble with?

Henning became aware of the pronounced silence
and looked around sharply. Everybody turned away
or looked down at the ground. There was a painful
pause. He must have felt that the silence was a direct
accusation, for suddenly he swung himself up on the
edge of the wall.

"Henning!" shouted Max fearfully. He thought
that Henning was going to jump down into the
arena. The Black Knight and the Mute were standing
quite close to the cellar door. Next to them stood Buffalo Bill with the big key in his hand.

"Buffalo Bill!" shouted Henning.

A whole group of preppies had left their places by
the wall and were heading towards the exit on the
other side of the yard. They were fooling around,
making a racket, but Henning's voice cut through
the commotion, and, after a few seconds, the noise
and yelling died completely down. Everybody looked
up at Henning who stood right on the lip of the wall.
For a moment he was completely motionless, like a
statue, but then he moved—he raised his arm and
pointed at the Black Knight. In the space between
his stillness and the moment he moved, I had the

strange feeling that he was suspended in an ancient, invisible silence which he had to fight his way through.

"I, Henning, challenge the Black Knight!"

His words echoed through the yard; you could hear the pride and dignity in them. I, Henning! A moment's surprise and astonishment—and then a storm of wild applause! The preppies roared with happiness and triumph; they danced around, clapped their hands, shouted at each other. I stood there feeling superior just because I knew Henning, we lived in the same yard!

But the Black Knight was totally indifferent to the preppies' enthusiasm. He turned his face towards us, the black mask effectively hiding whatever he might have been feeling—eagerness, fear, anger or satisfaction. Buffalo Bill turned towards the Black Knight and pulled at his brown forelock, not sure of what to do. At the same time Henning called out as if victory was already filling his voice:

"Black Knight! Do you accept my challenge?"

After a few seconds the Black Knight nodded and raised the sharp, gleaming point of his lance towards Henning. Then he and the Mute went through the tin door and were swallowed by the darkness inside the cellar. Buffalo Bill carefully locked the door after them.

The preppies were ecstatic.

Henning had challenged the Black Knight! And the Black Knight had accepted! When Henning hopped down from the wall, he was immediately mobbed by elated preppies slapping him on the back and praising him.

"The Black Knight doesn't have a chance!" said Christer, letting his hand rest on Henning's shoulder. Henning smiled; he looked both pleased and relieved. Karla Street, Grand Street, Nils-Wilhelm—all were forgotten, Henning was the hero of the day. Finally the Black Knight would be beaten; finally they'd tear off his mask as he lay on the ground half-conscious after Henning's awesome blow.

Swarming around Henning, they nearly carried him out in triumph across the yard, out through the door and into the street. The children of the yard went back to jumping rope and playing ball. But I lagged behind. Who *was* Henning going to get for a horse? He really was too heavy for me. And anyway, I didn't want to be that close to him, I didn't want to carry his body on my back. I could admire him, envy him, but I'd never be able to feel the same kind of warmth for him that I felt for Max.

When I came out into the street it was like coming back to reality, to an everyday world which I'd almost forgotten because the experience with the Black Knight had been so intense. Trucks chugged by, you could hear milk bottles rattling in the dairy stores, and at the bus stop people were fanning out in all directions towards home. Twilight already filled the spaces between the tall buildings.

Two lines of preppies—the fans of the Karla and

Grand Street Knights—walked up either side of the broad street. They'd started bantering again, and now they tried to shout down each other and the traffic. I could hardly hear their shrill shouts and strings of cursing. "Stuff it up your ass, you losers . . . Long live Christer!" was all I heard above the squeaking trams, the honking car horns, and the jingling bicycle bells.

"Karla Street wears green . . ."

Karla Knights? Grand Street Knights? I felt as though I'd been part of something that had happened a long time ago, something grand and colorful and heroic, and something which now, like a weak echo from the past, was being kept alive by the shouting, barely visible knights.

And then, suddenly, the knights disappeared. All I could hear as I stood alone on the street in the throng of people were isolated single notes. Yet it seemed to me that the words had a strange glow and luster as if they came from a more exciting and bold era:

> *Karla Street has won the day,*
> *Christer led us in the fray;*
> *Victory is ours to hold,*
> *Our lances strong, our knights so bold!*

9

I was free after my last class in school, but Henning and Max had their afternoons and evenings completely regulated, and God help them if they didn't pay attention to every tick of the clock. Neither the general nor the banker believed in sparing the rod.

After they'd done their homework, however, they could come down to the yard for a while. They'd sit in their favorite place by the old oak with their backs facing the front house so that they were hidden by the trunk and the foliage, and the housemaids would have to yell out the windows to find them. First came the piping voice of the general's housemaid three floors up, and then the maid with the Varmland accent from the banker's family cried cheerfully, "Ma-ax, Ma-ax, time for dinner!"

"I guess the people in the front house all eat at the same time," I'd say at home as I stood nosing around in the pantry for something to eat.

60

"High-class people always eat at certain hours," Mother said. "It's good for the digestion."

"That's how they do *everything*," Poppa added. "Even you know what. That's why they don't have very many kids!"

When they sat by the tree trunk Henning and Max would talk almost all the time about Ostra Prep. I'd hang around them doing exercises, and sometimes I'd clamber up into the tree and swing on a strong, springy, low-hanging limb. They didn't have anything against my listening; actually, my presence made them feel important. They knew that their world, the one they painted with their words, was much more eventful and colorful than my meager one in junior high school.

The teachers, for instance.

We had just one teacher for all subjects except shop, while they had different ones for each subject. The subjects themselves had more elegant names than ours: Physics, Biology, and Chemistry instead of our old-fashioned Science; Mathematics instead of our Arithmetic. It was only natural for us to take it for granted that there was more than just a difference in names, and that their knowledge was somehow deeper and truer than ours. And they spoke so casually about their teachers. They even gave them nicknames: the Swedish teacher was "the Slave Driver" (he failed you for the slightest misspelling); "Itchy" was the history teacher (he had a nervous habit of scratching himself behind the ear); and the speech teacher was "Mus" because he was supposed to be as exacting as Mussolini himself.

Max was the biggest gossip in the school. He knew who'd gotten his ears boxed, his nose pulled, or a black mark in the grade book for fooling around.

"And then Mayflower said, 'Do you want a beating or a demerit?' 'A demerit, sir,' said Nicholas, because his father was away. 'Okay, you've got it, but first you'll get a beating for being stupid enough to want a demerit instead of a beating!' Can you believe it? Nicholas really got the short end of the stick that time!"

They spoke foreign languages too. When they threw around German verbs and prepositions I became even more aware of the gap which would separate us in the future. The preppies would walk in their fathers' footsteps and become generals, judges, doctors, civil engineers—worldly, sophisticated, well-paid. And we from the regular public school—what would we become except delivery boys, stock room boys, unskilled laborers?

For instance, when I read *Ivanhoe* I had to guess what the foreign words in italics meant, the kind of words Buffalo Bill used during the tournament. *Largesse*—that had something to do with generosity. But I couldn't imagine what *Beauséant* or *desdichado* meant, and I didn't dare ask Henning or Max for fear of showing my ignorance even more. A battle *à outrance* meant a fight with bare weapons, with sharp lance tips instead of the wooden covers they used in

62

real tournaments (of course Buffalo Bill used cork ones). But what *à outrance* really meant I found out by something that happened right after the tournament.

As we were leaving Buffalo Bill's yard after the Black Knight's victory, a preppie walking in front of me turned and said, "It was lucky that . . ." But he stopped when he saw who I was—a public school kid—and got all flustered.

He spotted Max several meters away, and he said to him in a voice filled with relief, "It was lucky for Nils-Wilhelm that they didn't have a fight *à outrance*, to the bitter end! If they had, the Black Knight would have run him through!"

À outrance—to the bitter end, a fight to the death!

Later in the fall when the leaves turned red and yellow and darkness fell quickly, Henning and Max wouldn't hang out very much in the yard. They'd have a lot more homework to do, and the lessons they took on the side would begin—dancing, fencing, piano, marksmanship. None of the housemaids would stick her head out the kitchen window to shout: "Time for dinner!"

But the day after Henning's challenge, I was out in the yard as usual after school. I was competing against myself in the standing broad jump; sometimes I wished there was a kid my own age in the backhouse instead of all the little kids I was always stumbling over.

Though Henning and Max would usually come down at the same time because Max would knock on Henning's door on his way down, today Henning came out first—alone. He looked around. I thought he was looking for Max.

"Max isn't around," I said.

"I know," he answered curtly.

He sat down in his place by the tree trunk. A moment later Max came out and sat next to him. But every time someone walked across the yard, Henning looked up to see who it was.

The September day was warm and lazy with the smell of afternoon coffee floating through the yard. Sleepy flies and wasps buzzed around slowly, and small birds rustled in the foliage. From the wooden carpet rack came the clear voices of little children talking about someone's mother who'd seen a headless ghost one winter night.

"A ghost has to have a head," said one of the girls. "Otherwise it isn't really a ghost."

"I know how the Black Knight can be beaten," Henning said after Max started to talk about the challenge. Max often did other people's worrying for them.

"I know how the Black Knight can be beaten," Henning repeated. He was drawing something on the ground with a long stick he'd found—lines which were either parallel or crossing each other, like a battle plan. "The most important thing is the attack. You have to use the horse's attacking strength; he's got to

64

be a weapon himself, or at least a weapon bearer. And the rider is the weapon holder. Nils-Wilhelm had almost no attack at all—he practically just stood still. The attack is what the whole thing's about . . . you saw how fast the Mute was, right?"

"But who are you going to get for a horse?" said Max, annoyed that Henning wasn't even dealing with the most important point. "All we have is Roland, and you're too heavy for him. Or maybe you're going to use Roland anyway? Roland, go and start lifting weights to build the hell up!"

"I don't want Roland," Henning answered. Since the discussion was partly about me, this time I didn't have to swing in the trees like Tarzan. I came down and joined them.

"So who *are* you going to get?" Max persisted. "There isn't anybody else. The horse has to come from the same yard as you do. And you can't cheat. I don't know how you expect to fight the Black Knight without a horse!"

"I'm not going to fight him without a horse. I know who I want. I've been thinking about it for a very long time." He spoke with real intensity.

"Oh you have? So maybe there's some family that's going to move in during the next few days? Maybe some sergeant's family with a big, strapping kid who can carry you?"

"Nobody's moving in."

"So who *is* it then? Come on, Henning!"

"Someone who's absolutely perfect. Someone who

nobody has thought about. Not you, not Roland, not anyone."

"*Who is it?!*" Max and I were so impatient we said it in unison. Henning answered calmly.

"Kossan."

We stared in amazement.

"Kossan? But she's a girl!"

It was obvious that he meant it. He nodded and repeated, "Kossan. Nobody said that the horse couldn't be a girl, did they?"

10

Kossan!

She was a girl our age who lived with her mother on the top floor of the backhouse in an apartment above us. An extraordinarily big and stocky girl with powerful arms and legs, she was a redhead, but her hair wasn't really a bright red—it was more sort of muddy and dull. And she had freckles all over her face, not those cute girlish freckles, the kind that are sort of sprinkled over the bridge of the nose. No, Kossan's freckles were ugly, and they covered her whole face as if she had some kind of skin disease. Her teeth, however, were regular and white, which was a little unusual for people like us; most of the people I knew were pretty careless about brushing their teeth.

Kossan.

Her nickname had the same mysterious origin as the nicknames of the teachers at Ostra Prep; nobody knew exactly where it came from. Everybody called her Kossan (which in Swedish is sort of the same as

"Elsie the Cow") and had always called her that. Whether she'd gotten the nickname because she was as heavy and ungainly as a cow, as dumb as a cow, or for some other reason (maybe her real name *was* Elsie!), no one bothered to find out.

Her mother was a thin little lady who worked as a telephone operator at the south switchboard on Hogbergs Street. Rumor had it that she was from a "better" family (she never shopped on credit like the rest of us), but her family had kicked her out when they'd found out that the child's father was an ordinary dock worker who was already married to someone else. Shame and damnation!

"No wonder she's shy," said Mom. "Being an illegitimate kid and everything."

"Aw, kids don't worry about things like that," Poppa declared. "The problem is that her mother doesn't have any life in her. She'd hold it in the whole night before she'd disturb the neighbors by flushing the toilet. That's what I call being considerate to the dead. How can the kid be anything *but* shy?"

My parents considered themselves a step better than Kossan's mother even though they'd had three kids (including me!) before they'd finally gotten married.

"Oh, you know, we had our ups and downs," said Mom. "And of course I was always looking for the right man. A couple of kids wouldn't have mattered, but if I'd been married . . . !"

Kossan and I went to the same public school, so we saw each other during recess. Otherwise, I avoided talking to her because Olle might just put his two cents in and say, "Hey, Roland's got himself a broad. He's crazy about Kossan!"

When she was in the yard, she'd stick close to the carpet rack playing with the little kids or having a catch with herself with two worn-out tennis balls. Actually, she had a real feeling for ball games: during the summer she and I played boxball together, and most of the time her steadiness and determination overpowered me.

As Henning and Max sat by their tree and I swung on my limb listening to them, she'd stand near me tossing the balls gently in the air. But never for long. It was as if she wanted to show us that she wasn't trying to be pushy, and so she'd go back to the carpet rack no matter how much she seemed to be interested in the conversation.

One thing irritated me: Kossan read a lot. Sometimes I'd stop her as she came back from the library and I'd look over the books she'd borrowed. I'd criticize her choices—it was sort of expected—but as fast as I could I'd borrow the same books and read them no matter how boring they were, just so she couldn't tell me anything. *I* was the one who read books. I was the one who was supposed to show off to her about all the books I'd read. And even though neither she nor I owned a blessed thing, I'd staked a claim on reading books the same way a prospector stakes a claim on a mine. So what right did she have fooling around in my territory?

Something else which got me even angrier was that while I raced through the stuff I read and came out with only a general idea of the people and the milieu, she remembered ideas and names—who said this, who did that. I could never make sayings out of the things I'd read the way she could: "I just ate and drank like 1728 Lilliputians." For me reading was like getting drunk. Though I never did forget names and titles.

Like the rest of us, Kossan had been fascinated by *Ivanhoe*. She was very curious about Buffalo Bill's tournament and the Black Knight, and she had her own theory about why the Black Knight wore a mask. "It's harder to beat him that way," she said. "His opponents get scared. They don't know what he's hiding behind the mask. If he didn't have a mask, people would say, 'Aw, that's only Anders,' and they wouldn't be afraid of him anymore."

"He's not wearing the mask just to scare people," I'd say. "He's hiding something under it. Can you imagine Henning putting on a mask just to scare people?"

"Henning's different. He's the best!"

She kept asking how much it cost to get into Buffalo Bill's tournament even though, as the poorest of us, she never had *any* money. Just as my parents considered themselves a cut above her unmarried mother, I was a cut above her because I usually had enough money to go to Sunday afternoon matinees.

70

When I'd come back from the movies she'd always be outside the door waiting for me to tell her all about it. And to bug her I wouldn't say anything for a long time, or else I'd talk about something else so that she'd finally have to say, "Did you go to the movies? What did you see?"

"How much does it cost to get into the tournament?"

"You can't get in. It's only for preppies," I answered. "Anyway, you don't have a cent."

"Olle and the others get in."

"They're horses, dummy. They get a good deal. First they get paid to be horses, then they can see the Black Knight for free."

Today, shortly before Henning had come out, Kossan had stopped to watch me practice broad jumping. She'd been on her way to the dairy store and stood swinging her empty milk bottle slowly; with her powerful build and big red hands she looked like a milkmaid on the way to milk her cows.

In school she'd heard that I'd been to the tournament the day before and had seen the Black Knight defeat Nils-Wilhelm. Henning's challenge was the big news of the day, even bigger than the fact that the AIK soccer team had won.

"You said that only preppies could get in," she said slightly accusingly. And I answered, feeling more than a little proud, "I was with Henning and Max, that's why I got in. You should have heard Henning

71

challenge the Black Knight! It was fabulous! Henning's the only one in the world who can beat him. And you should have seen the Black Knight! My heart almost stopped, my hair stood on end!"

She couldn't hear enough about the tournament, or about Christer of the Karla Street Knights and the hush that had fallen when the Black Knight came into the arena. When she'd get interested in something, her shyness would vanish and her face would get softer and livelier. All of her changed, really; you could hardly recognize her. It felt great to act superior to her, and it annoyed me to think that maybe there was another girl inside plain Kossan, a clear-thinking, bright girl with a sharp, alert look, someone without guile, deceit or phoniness.

"Are you going to be Henning's horse?" she asked; she knew that horse and rider had to come from the same yard.

"I'll see," I answered coolly. "Run and buy your milk. Yesterday it was all gone by now. Mom had to buy beer instead."

Yes, I was about ready to be Henning's horse even if he was too heavy for me. Horses earned money, and I needed money to buy the "O" model Erector set. Or at the very least, the "OO." An Erector set— that was pure bliss!

And now Kossan would be Henning's horse!

As usual, Max not only accepted Henning's idea; he praised him for it.

"Kossan! Yeah, she's solid as a rock. What a brilliant idea, Henning! Only you could have thought it up! A girl for a horse! Wait till the Black Knight sees it—he'll fall off his horse in shock. What do you think, Roland?"

"Kossan's very interested in the tournament. She's been wondering who Henning's horse was going to be."

Just at that moment Kossan came back from the dairy. She made a little detour around the oak so as not to disturb us and headed towards the backhouse. Henning followed her attentively, sizing her up with his eyes.

"Call her," he said to me.

"Kossan!" I shouted.

She stopped abruptly.

"Come here."

Obediently she came towards us. Her dull red hair was somewhere in between curly and straight. She avoided looking directly at us; her eyes focused somewhere around our stomachs.

"You're going to be my horse," Henning said. "I challenged the Black Knight and I'm going to beat him. You're the only one who can carry me. I'm too heavy for Roland. It's a matter of personal honor for me and for the whole yard."

"And the horses get paid," Max added anxiously. "So that they'll do their best."

She looked up, met Henning's scrutinizing eyes, and her face turned beet red. She dropped her eyes

73

quickly and mumbled, "I'd do my best even if I didn't get paid!"

Dumb Kossan! The one person in the whole world who never had any money!

"You'll be paid the going rate," said Henning. It sounded very official—the "going rate."

"I just have to run upstairs with the milk," she said, and held out the milk bottle and bag and spun on her heels and took off like a rocket through the door.

"I'll bet you anything she doesn't come down again. She'll lock herself in till winter," Max said. "She's just like all girls—chicken."

But she came back almost immediately. She must have just put the stuff in the apartment and run back down the stairs. Out of breath and nervous, she looked like she was afraid that Henning had changed his mind.

"Do you really want me to be your horse? Do you think I can do it?"

We'd seen her play horse many times before. At the carpet rack the little kids would climb on her back and she'd carry them around the yard and they'd throw their arms around her neck and shriek with a mixture of fear and delight to find themselves so high off the ground. Sometimes she'd gallop, back and forth, back and forth, and the howling would grow even louder.

It was possible Henning had gotten the idea to use her as a horse as she galloped around the yard with

74

that gang of kids behind her. But it could be that a paragraph from *The Condor* had stuck in his memory. Jonas Fjeld had ridden at the head of a small expedition in the jungle on a saddled cow. A cow! And what was good enough for the great Jonas Fjeld was even good enough for Henning.

11

Henning had to fight the Black Knight whether he wanted to or not.

As the leader of the preppies he was feared as well as admired, and it was almost unreal how infallible he was, how completely superior to everyone else. When he'd finally challenged the Black Knight it was only what everybody had been expecting. Finally the mysterious Black Knight would meet his match; finally everyone would find out which preppie was hiding behind the black mask! Or . . . maybe not. Had the people who wanted Henning to lose joined in the cheering too, the people who wanted to see Henning lying outstretched on the ground, finally defeated?

As a boy the General, Henning's father, had been first in everything, and he insisted that Henning be the same. Henning had to show all his tests to his father, and if he didn't get every single thing right, his father would be furious. What was wrong with him? Hadn't he studied? Was he dumb, apathetic, lazy?

Whenever he competed in something, he had to be the best in his division; that was taken for granted. Hadn't his father been the decathlon champion of Sweden? They hardly had any conversations; it was all just question-and-answer and giving orders. A man wasn't supposed to talk much; he was just supposed to know what he wants and then pass the order down to a flunky who'll carry it out right away without question.

Henning didn't have anything like Max's sunny, happy disposition. But when he felt more than usually oppressed by his father's demands, he'd look really gloomy and become even more silent and self-absorbed; then you'd know that something had happened to awaken the general's displeasure.

"Henning is supposed to be a general too," said Max. "Luckily his father isn't the Commander of the Armed Forces; that might be hard for Henning to match. Or maybe he could become a Swedish Napoleon and conquer all of Europe! His father would like that. *My* father too! We could open banks in all the capitals! I'd take the one in Paris!"

Like the rest of us, Henning didn't have much use for girls; they were just something to be tolerated. In his case, though, it wasn't so strange, because Henning went with his father to masculine places (fencing matches, expositions, swimming pools)—a world filled with manly deeds, bravery, courage. A woman's place was in the home; that he could see with his own eyes. Little girls were brought up to keep house and give orders to maids, cooks and nursemaids.

That's why we thought it was perfectly natural for Kossan to stand waiting and hoping that Henning hadn't changed his mind about giving her the honor of being his horse. There was never a question of what *she* wanted, only if Henning would accept her as a horse or not.

He walked around Kossan and inspected her the way a general inspects his troops, still holding the stick in his hands and every once in a while slapping it against his thigh like a riding crop. With a critical frown on his face he looked at her black, worn shoes and said, "She has to have other shoes. Sneakers."

"Run up and change," said Max.

She blushed again; that was something she did easily. And she stuttered in embarrassment:

"I-I-I can't wear sneakers d-during the week. Only for athletics. That's what my m-m-mother says."

While she talked Henning looked suprised, as though he thought that she was a real horse. But it was the kind of thing that he and Max understood too; parents' commands were law. Finally Max ran upstairs and got an old used pair that he'd been thinking of throwing away anyway. She tried them on, and they fit perfectly. Max was totally amazed.

"How strange! She's taller than I am! But she can still get into my sneakers."

Then Henning ordered her to run around the yard

several times; he wanted to see how fast she was. I'd never seen her run like that—she sped around in the sneakers, taking long, sure strides. When she stopped short in front of him, she was breathing only a little more quickly than before.

"It's the sneakers that did it!" she said.

Henning ran his hand through his blond hair and looked at the blue sneakers as though he thought they had wings. Then he grunted and decided to try to sit on her back.

Two wide stairs led up to the door to the backhouse. He got up on the higher one, shooed away some inquisitive flies and climbed on Kossan's back. Leaning slightly forward, she grabbed hold of his legs at the knees. While he held her shoulder with one hand, she stood completely still, her legs straight, and stared straight at the ground.

"Let's go," he hissed, and touched her with his stick on her other shoulder. She took a few steps forward, then he squeezed her shoulder and she stopped.

"It's a really good seat," he announced in surprise.

Max and I gaped at the two of them. Kossan carried Henning as though he were as light as a feather; her face was red not with strain, but excitement. We could never have dreamed that Henning would look that impressive: he towered over us, as if he were really sitting on a horse. Both of them looked so solid—solid, massive, powerful.

"Is he heavy?" I asked.

She shook her head.

"Trot over to the carpet rack," Henning commanded, and she jogged obediently over to it, looking even happier than one evening when I gave her a worn, beat-up copy of Jack London's *The People of the Abyss* that my sister had pinched from the cafe where she worked. "Roland!" she'd said. "Jack London! That's fantastic!"

Henning sat nonchalantly on her back, almost as if he were glued on; he didn't even need to hold onto her. At the carpet rack he gave her a new order: she turned and rushed at us full speed ahead, and we dove to the side, startled. They looked really dangerous! Kossan stopped short.

"That was fabulous," said Max.

Kossan stood still, hardly panting. Henning lifted both hands.

"Hey look," he seemed to be saying, "I'm higher than the Black Knight! I can thrust downwards! And I can use both hands at once! He's doomed!"

For the first time in a long time, his face lit up like the sun, and he smiled broadly. At first he'd tried to fight it and look very serious, but the feeling of future victory was too strong—it came from deep inside and pushed through with such force that he couldn't stop a smile from lighting up his sunburned, aristocratic face. He looked as pleased as punch. "Didn't I tell you?" his expression said.

"That was fabulous," Max repeated.

"You can let go," Henning commanded, and he

slid down to the ground. He looked so pleased that he was completely beside himself. Nothing happened for several seconds; we all just bathed in a wonderful feeling of solidarity. For the first time we felt that the four of us belonged together, that we were all part of a winning team, that the mysterious Black Knight was standing on the brink of defeat and the moment of his demasking was just around the corner.

"Did you see how she could charge! But, look, we've got to keep this a secret! Nobody should say a word about Kossan being the horse—it's got to come as a complete surprise! Remember, it's a secret!"

We nodded, overjoyed.

12

The idea of keeping it a secret appealed to all of us immensely. We just couldn't stop gloating to each other about how startled and surprised the preppies and the Black Knight would be when Henning entered the arena. And how Henning would defeat the Black Knight as easily and as playfully as the Black Knight had defeated Nils-Wilhelm.

It doesn't take any talent to keep a little secret, but this was a big, important one, and I had a lot of trouble keeping my mouth shut when Olle asked whom Henning was going to use as a horse. I was just on the verge of telling him that it was a big secret, but if I had Olle and Sixten and the others would have wormed the secret out of me before you know it. So I just grimaced in feigned disinterest: "I don't know. All I know is it's not me."

"You didn't tell anyone in school, did you?" I asked Kossan in a self-satisfied way as we arrived home together and pushed open the front door.

"Tell anyone?"

"That you're going to be Henning's horse."

She just stared wide-eyed at me. Henning had said that it was a secret: the thought of telling anyone hadn't even crossed her mind.

"What are you going to do with the money?" I asked.

"The money? If I get any, I'll save it."

"Save it? That's ridiculous! You know what I'd do? I'd buy an Erector set. The 'O' model. In Sigge's yard there's a preppie who's got the No. 4 model, the one with the motor. No. 4! With that one you can build a drawbridge or a windmill or a mechanical lift that goes up and down!"

I was depressed that she was going to make money and I wasn't. In school the horses were an envied group—they had money, we didn't. Some of them spent their money right away on candy, comic books, movies; others like Olle and Sixten saved it. Olle seemed to be obsessed about getting money any way he could. He wanted to buy a used bicycle, and even though this was a fairly remote goal, he was incredibly single-minded, and the only luxury he allowed himself was an occasional movie matinee. Sixten had an even grander goal: he put all *his* money in a cigar box on which he had written, MONEY FOR MY TRIP TO AMERICA. He wanted to go to San Francisco and dig for gold and see the earthquakes and eat food with chopsticks. We used to kid him.

"How's your saving going, Sixten? Maybe you'll have enough to take the trolley to Slussen soon. Then they can tell you how to get to Chinatown from there!"

As a rule, Kossan and I finished school earlier than our two preppies, but neither of us really considered sitting in their places by the tree trunk. I had my bough and Kossan had the little kids to play with. Today she ran around with them playing hide-and-seek in among the wash hanging out on long lines; kids peeked out from behind sheets and handkerchiefs and long underwear. Then, after they tired of that game, they wanted her to be the teacher and play school with them; she'd found a pair of eyeglass frames without the glasses which made her look about 100 years old.

Finally, later than usual, Henning and Max arrived. They'd been busy making a costume more spectacular than Nils-Wilhelm's. Henning would wear his own "noble" colors—gold and red—with the emphasis on the gold.

"Gold is the color of winners," he explained. "And red is the color of life, the color of blood pulsing in your veins."

He wanted a tunic made out of goldlike material; he'd been looking for a chain-mail vest his father had used one time in fencing, but Max had found something made out of gold lamé in his mother's closet. The collar of the costume would be red.

"The Golden Knight—that's what you'll be!"

Henning was in an exceptionally good mood, and at one point he asked Kossan to run around with the

little kids on her back just to warm up a little. He
and Max worked on the helmet. They'd found a hat
without a brim that they reinforced with cardboard,
and they were discussing whether they should cover
it with gold paper or paint it gold.

"What are you going to use for a lance?" I asked.
Strengthened by yesterday's sense of unity, I'd crept
close to them.

Henning explained that he had a javelin that he'd
used in school athletics. It had split, but he thought
he could glue it together and perhaps shorten it
several inches. A real lance should also have a
hand-guard, but in this case it would be unneces-
sary.

"But the javelin's cracked," Max objected.

"I said I'll glue it together. It'll hold for one thrust,
and that's all we'll need. We'll paint it gold too."

They went inside, and I looked over to Kossan.
Why hadn't I thought of using Kossan as a horse? I
could dress exactly like the Black Knight—in white,
of course—because then I wouldn't have to do so
much painting. I'd have a white face mask and a
white lance. And everybody would hold his breath
when I entered the arena—the Black Knight against
the White Knight. Kossan would have to have a mask
too so that no one would recognize her; otherwise,
they'd be able to figure out who the White Knight
was. And I'd charge the Black Knight at full speed
and jab my lance at him and he'd go flying out of his
saddle and I'd tear off my mask and everyone would
shout in amazement:

"Look! It's Roland Andersson! He lives in Henning's yard! He's defeated the Black Knight!"

And I'd get a whole pile of money for my victory and finally I'd be able to buy the "O" model Erector set!

13

The next day Henning and Max came down with the half-finished helmet and the javelin which they planned to use as a lance. It was a long wooden one with a steel point, and it was wrapped with tape in the middle. You could see the split in it, but Henning had glued it together and let it dry overnight.

"It's too long and clumsy. But if I cut off some in back, it'll get top heavy and that would be a shame because it's beautifully balanced. Here, feel it!" And to my surprise (for usually he was very finicky about his possessions), he handed the javelin to me. It felt heavier than I'd thought it would be.

"Y-yes, it's very well balanced," I agreed.

If he cut some off both ends, he'd have to make a new point, and you couldn't really do something like that overnight. So while he tried to decide what to do, he tested his strength by throwing the javelin across the yard; Kossan was told to keep the kids out of the way over by the carpet rack.

Suddenly we all heard a cheery "Hi!" from a familiar voice. Rebecca came through the door from the front house, and right on her heels was Buffalo Bill carrying a rectangular carton under his arm. I'd only seen him in his cape, and I was a little surprised to see that without it he just looked like an ordinary kid.

Henning leaned the javelin against the oak tree. He gave Max and me a warning glance—Don't say a thing about Kossan! The two of them came up to us, and Buffalo Bill shook everybody's hand. Max sat against the tree making a half-hearted attempt to conceal the helmet in his hands.

"I see you're making a magic helmet," said Rebecca. "Is that your secret weapon?"

With her green scarf tied loosely around her neck, she looked more beautiful than ever; she wasn't as frisky as usual, and it seemed to suit her better.

"Magic helmet?"

"You know, like in *Siegfried*. A helmet made out of gold. You become invisible when you put it on. If the Black Knight would get one too, then it'd really be a fight. Two lances fumbling around in the air by themselves!"

"What did you come here for?" said Henning. I thought he sounded almost unfriendly.

"To pay my cousin Max the money I borrowed the other day. I can't afford paying his interest rates. And Buffalo Bill came to . . . Oh, Henning, you actually won!" she interrupted herself impulsively, unable to stifle a giggle.

"Won? Won what?"

Buffalo Bill looked like he'd been cheated out of making his grand announcement. But he collected his wits immediately.

"The xylophone. According to the drawing in Buffalo Bill's American Lottery, the first prize—a xylophone made by Melochord, the world-famous xylophone maker—goes to lottery ticket No. 95. Here it is!"

"It's never been touched by human hands," said Rebecca. "And made by the famous Melancholy Manufacturing Company . . . I was even the one who chose the ticket! I went to the drawing to make sure they did everything right—and I picked your number! What do you think that means?"

"It means I'm a born winner."

He took the xylophone out of the gray carton. A little stand on four skinny legs went with it, and there were mallets attached too. Squatting, Henning went up and down the scales a few times, then played a short marching tune with hard, mechanical precision.

"Almost two octaves," he said, and he gathered up the equipment and put it back in the carton. That was more like him: he'd take possession of something and make it his, and then wouldn't allow anyone else to get near it.

Rebecca wanted to try the javelin, but Henning pulled it away. "Let go! I just glued it together! It could come apart again."

"Glued it together? All the Black Knight needs to do is blow on it for it to break in a million pieces. For that matter, all he needs to do is blow on you, too . . . So if Roland's not going to be your horse, who is?"

Henning had let the other preppies know that he wasn't going to use me as his horse, but he hadn't told them anything else. It wasn't a problem for him to keep a secret.

"It's a secret," Max said.

We were standing under the tree branches which formed a roof of leaves over us. A soft breeze blew caressingly through the wash hanging out to dry in the right hand corner of the yard. By the carpet rack, Kossan's school (with her as teacher, her eyeglasses on her nose) was still in progress. Nobody thought she was even worth a glance; they acted as if she didn't exist. She was just some girl with little kids around her.

"I need one more Nameless Knight," said Buffalo Bill. "If Roland could be Max's horse, we'd have a complete team to go against Grand Street."

"You can get up a team some other way," Max complained. "I absolutely refuse! I just want to sit back and watch the Black Knight lose. . . . And anyway, who's going to handle the betting?"

"There's plenty of time for that. The jousting doesn't take very long. And it's an honor to be a Nameless Knight. An honor where you can make some money too!"

Henning was leaning against the tree trunk. His upper body was bent slightly forward, and his chin rested on his hands which held the long javelin. He looked like an illustration out of a saga, his blond hair shining brightly in the leafy dimness; Rebecca looked at him but didn't say anything.

"Max will be a Nameless Knight. And Roland will be his horse," Henning finally said in a voice that allowed no disagreement. Max gave him a gloomy look and turned his lips outward in a pout. Buffalo Bill wrote our names in his book; I tried to look blasé, but I felt a surge of expectation and joy—finally I'd earn some money too!

"Who's going to be your horse, Henning?"

Rebecca looked up at the windows of the backhouse as if she expected some boy to stick out his head and shout, "I am!"

"It's a secret," answered Henning, and we nodded.

"The Secret Club," snorted Rebecca. "So keep your old secret. The Black Knight will probably make mincemeat out of you and your secret horse anyway. How much do I owe you, Max?"

"Everyone thinks I know who the Black Knight is," complained Buffalo Bill as he sat cross-legged on the ground; Max and Rebecca went off a few steps to transact their business. "But I don't," he continued. "On my word of honor."

"Maybe the Black Knight is the Black Knight!" Rebecca burst out.

"What's that supposed to mean? Of course he is!"

"No, I mean the *real* Black Knight. Richard the Lionhearted who's come out of the Deepest Darkness to make fools of the kids from Ostra Prep."

"Then he's shrunk quite a lot!"

"People were much smaller in the Middle Ages; they've gotten much bigger since then. Once when I was on a trip with my parents, I saw a suit of armor that Carl the Great wore. He wasn't any taller than me, and still they called him Carl the Great!"

"Henning thinks it's Uno," said Max. "The guy who broke his leg last spring and hasn't been able to walk right since. The Mute always carries him into the arena—do you realize that nobody's ever seen the Black Knight on foot?"

"He could be a grown-up," said Rebecca. "A dwarf maybe, like the Hunchback of Notre Dame."

"He was a hunchback, not a dwarf!" said Henning. "A dwarf is small. The Black Knight isn't that small."

"Well, maybe an unusually *big* dwarf then!"

"The Black Knight is only in our imagination," suggested Max. "Mr. Ohlander says that life is an illusion, a fantasy. We see the Black Knight because we *want* to see him."

"An illusion? Tell that to Nils-Wilhelm. . . . What do you think, Roland?"

"I don't know," I said timidly. Buffalo Bill didn't make fun of my response, and it made me feel warm and happy when he said, " 'I don't know.' That's a sensible attitude. Just imagine if people said that instead of pretending to know things when they don't."

As far as I was concerned, the four of them could sit there and talk as long as they liked; it felt both exciting and soothing. They talked in a way that was completely different from my friends in school—quicker, but always clear, direct, and to the point. They were also friendlier to each other than we were—we put each other down all the time. It was always a battle just to hold your own, to keep other people from getting the best of you.

"You know what people are saying?" Max said eagerly. "They're saying that the Black Knight's gloves are electrified. He's got a battery inside his clothes and wires leading up through his lance to the metal tip so that when someone gets hit, they get such a shock they're almost knocked off their horse!"

"What about the cork cones I put on? The current can't go through cork. It's not a conductor."

"Still, it's not a bad idea," said Rebecca. "Why don't you hollow out your lance, Henning, and fill it with ink? Then you could just push a button and pow! Ink all over the Black Knight so he couldn't see his nose! That should take care of him."

"He'll be taken care of anyway," Henning said.

"You could get a lead lance," said Max. "Then, when you dropped it on the Mute's toes, he'd dance around and the Black Knight would go flying off!"

"I think he's one of our mortal enemies," said Buffalo Bill. "You know, when the Mute comes to pick up the money for the Black Knight, he just puts out his paw, grunts and gives me a typewritten note: AN-

93

OTHER POMPOUS ASS OF AN OSTRA PREPPIE BITES THE
DUST! Pompous ass! Now who but a kid from North
Latin would think up something like that?"

Buffalo Bill had never told any of them this before,
and they all thought it over in gloomy silence. It
really sounded as though it were a guy from North
Latin.

"Was it in Swedish or Latin?" Rebecca asked.

"I don't think there's a single kid who'd know how
to say 'pompous ass' in Latin!"

"It could be one of your teachers," said Rebecca.
"Just think what fun it would be for him to beat you
anonymously, one after the other."

Max looked up at the sky and sighed. Girls!

"They don't need to do it anonymously. They can
do it right out in the open. Uffe got such a slap from
Sahlin that he went around with five fingers on his
face for hours. Then Nero in geography (he's a little
nearsighted anyway) told him to take his hand away
from his cheek. 'It isn't my hand, sir. It's Mr. Sahlin's. And it won't come off.' No, they really hit us
hard—that's the difference between girls' schools and
boys' schools."

"Oh really? There was this one time I was supposed to sing a solo in front of the music teacher, and
I told her she'd played a wrong note. 'I have perfect
pitch,' I said. 'Nonsense,' she said. 'You know what
I see?' And she stared angrily at me through the music stand with all that grating stuff on it. 'I see a
monkey in the zoo.' 'So do I,' I said, and then she
raised her hand to give me a smack but changed her

mind and hit the top of the piano so hard it echoed all through the room. Then she marched out, even though we still had five minutes left."

"That wasn't very polite of you," said Henning.

"Polite of *me*? What about her?"

"Well, you do look like a monkey, don't you?"

"Do you want five fingers on your cheek too?"

She smiled for an instant, then bounced nimbly to her feet.

"I've got to go now. I was going to borrow 448,365 kronor from Max. Don't look like such a dummy, Buffalo Bill. It's the name of a book, Jonas Fjeld's first adventure, *448,365 Kronor!*"

"Oh, him. You know, you live in a dream world. You talk about Jonas Fjeld as if he really exists. Talk about illusions! Anyway, you can't call a book *448 . . .* whatever it was."

"Come with me up to Max's place and you'll see."

"Of course Jonas Fjeld really exists," said Max. "He's a Norwegian doctor. A good guy. In *The Condor* he breaks up a strike of dockworkers in Gothenberg—that's the kind of guy I want to meet."

But Rebecca knew whom *she* wanted to meet.

"Richard Arlen. He's going to be in the movie at the Sibyll Street Theater. *Santa Fe Trail*. I just hope he really acts like a cowboy instead of one of those boring, wooden heroes."

They shuffled over to the door to the front house to go up to Max's apartment. As he said goodbye, Buffalo Bill shook my hand.

"Hey, Roland, it's great that you'll be Max's horse.

Now you can earn some money for the soapbox car."

There was something charming and attractive about him. You could never really get mad at him; he was always interested in anybody he was talking to, and he was just as far from a pompous ass preppie as you could get. I really liked him.

"Why do I have to be a Nameless Knight?" complained Max in a low voice, looking quickly over at Buffalo Bill and Rebecca.

"I need someone to practice with," whispered Henning. "You and Roland can fight against me and Kossan—that way we'll all get practice."

All four vanished through the door into the front house.

The leaves rustled; the wind became stronger. Some clouds sailed over the rooftops, and you could feel a faint twinge of fall in the shadows. I felt lonely, and I looked across to the carpet rack and wondered how much Kossan had heard. The little kids were gone; she sat on the carpet rack, quietly, with folded hands.

"Who was that?" she asked when I came over.

"The master of ceremonies himself. Buffalo Bill. The one I told you about. Max is going to be a Nameless Knight because Henning needs practice."

"I heard," she said.

"So now I'm a horse too," I said, finally content. "I can save up enough for an Erector set."

14

The preppies may have had their own rooms, but Kossan and I had a lot more freedom than they did. We didn't have to do things by the clock, and we could stay out long after it got dark. Usually, though, we just hung around the yard by the cellar door. The stairs went down below ground level (unlike those in the front houses), and they left a space where you could sit privately, halfway underground.

I was the one who did most of the talking, and she was the one who listened. In my wanderings around Ostermalm I'd covered a lot of ground, and I had a lot of interesting things to talk about. But after she became Henning's horse, she wasn't satisfied just to throw in a word every once in a while—she became more talkative. Maybe she liked herself more because Henning had chosen her, or maybe she was just pleased to be allowed to be one of the boys.

On one of the last evenings before Henning's joust

with the Black Knight, we sat down by the cellar door as usual, hidden from the few people who walked by. In spite of the full moon shining over the rooftops, the yard was practically dark. The great oak seemed to absorb the moonlight and send it back with a ghostly glow. It was completely quiet; you couldn't even hear the Gramophone from the Ytterling's maid's window on the second floor.

"Olle hopes the tournament will keep going for a long while," I said. "He says it's like having a job."

Kossan and I agreed that it was pretty easy to be a horse; Max wasn't heavy at all.

"Just like a backpack with a few books, a thermos and some sandwiches," I said to Kossan. His legs were skinny, and I could easily reach around and clasp my hands across my stomach so that his knees would be locked in tight.

"What if I fall off?" he'd complain. "I could break my back!" And he certainly was scared of falling off; he'd almost lie down on my back and cling to me with both hands!

"Don't go so limp!" Henning would yell while we practiced. "Don't strangle Roland! Fight!" But Max went limp anyway when Henning and Kossan came charging towards us, Henning's gold lance raised menacingly (even though, of course, it wasn't for real); aside from his lance, the only part of his battle outfit that Henning was using was his helmet, and that was just to get used to it. But the suit was already finished, and with its red collar it looked really magnificent.

Max could hardly defend himself, and Henning would insist that he use both hands. But when Henning parried Max's lame, half-hearted thrusts—"Attack, Max, you've got to *attack!*"—Max would try to slife off. I could feel how he'd be struggling to get back on the ground, and finally I'd have to let him go. Henning seemed pleased anyway; it was perfectly natural to him that Max didn't have a chance of beating him.

Olle and Sixten used to kid me about being a horse for Max, one of the Nameless Knights who were supposed to fight Grand Street before Henning met the Black Knight.

"Scraping the bottom of the barrel, aren't you? Isn't Max that little nothing of a preppie? He doesn't look much like a knight!"

And even though I protested, secretly I agreed with them. He really *was* worthless. But I was just a horse, and, as Olle said, you had to treat it like a job. Pop carries shit-buckets, he'd snigger at me; I carry a preppie.

"I can't understand how Max can read Øvre Richter-Frisch," Kossan said. She was sitting on the lowest step with the top of her head just above ground, and she glanced nervously now and then up towards her own dark kitchen window. "Jonas Fjeld in that book is a . . . criminal, a real bully who doesn't like Jews. Anyway, what's so great about someone who beats up strikers?"

"You read him yourself."

"I read everything I can get my hands on, you know that. And it's still not enough. We read the same books!"

"Well, Jonas Fjeld is no criminal. He's a doctor. In *The Condor* he does an operation on Donna Francesca for tangled intestines."

"So why doesn't he get a job in a hospital instead of running all over the world killing people?"

"He doesn't kill people. He just kills bad guys."

"Yeah, the kind of people *he* thinks are bad guys."

"Well, what about Jack London then? He runs around all over the place. He's practically a bum."

"Jack London writes about things that really happen. He's been to the East End of London, and he's seen how poor people really live. He writes about the Monster of London who strangles children. One minute they're dancing to the song of the organ-grinder, playing, laughing—they're as good as the rich kids. But then the Monster gets them and you never see them again. They never get to be presidents or bankers, lawyers, engineers, generals—all the things rich kids become! The Monster swallows them up and turns them into stunted people, depressed people with ugly faces and dull brains. And that Monster is all over Stockholm too."

"It's not going to get me," I said, appalled. This new, talkative Kossan both irritated and fascinated me. She was supposed to keep quiet, to listen and blush and—at the very most—read books. And even though what she said was new to me, the seriousness in her voice made me feel older, more intelligent.

"And how are you going to manage that?" she said.

That moment was the first time in my life I stopped to think about my future. When I read books it was simple. There I lived right alongside my heroes: I was a genius like Captain Nemo, a doctor like Jonas Fjeld, a knight like Ivanhoe. But in reality I'd just finish public school one day, get a job as a delivery boy and slog through the Stockholm streets in all kinds of awful weather. The Monster would get to me too: slowly but surely it would strangle my dreams, stunt my ambitions, kill my hopes. I could build bridges and tunnels with the "O" model Erector set if I was lucky, but that's as far as it would go. The real future would be built by the rich kids, the ones with money, knowledge, power. An Erector set! It was a useful toy for the rich kids, something they could practice with until they got the real thing. Maybe that's why I wanted one so badly: it would make me feel like a rich kid, an illusion that the Stockholm Monster would soon drum out of me. The whole business made me feel dismal.

"I don't know," I answered curtly. "How are *you* going to do it?"

If you put a question to her, you could always be sure that she took it seriously; she didn't laugh it away or avoid answering it. That never ceased to amaze me.

"I'm going to be a teacher."

"A teacher? But that's a high-class profession!"

"I know. But I've got to do it. If only I can get the education. That's why Momma and I are saving, so

101

that I can, even though I think the government should pay for it. They should see that everyone gets an education, becomes what he wants to be, and does something good for society. Look at the preppies even! They're learning to be exactly like their fathers! I'm not so sure that Max should be a banker—maybe he'd like to be a vet instead. And he's just one example. I mean, what do you think life is really for?"

"That's easy!" I had an irresistible urge to lighten the conversation, and I suddenly remembered the sailor's words in *The People of the Abyss*:

"We live to drink and drink to live!"

She didn't say anything. The silvery-white light from the moon and the oak leaves fell over her, and you couldn't see the freckles on her wide face. Her eyes were shiny pools filled with drops of moonlight. Even her hair became different—dark red. A strange Kossan, almost beautiful.

I turned away, bewildered and confused by her sad expression after the joke I'd tried to make. A window slammed shut and a light came on in her house, in the kitchen. Still trying to keep the talk light, I almost said, "Well, at least your Mom didn't kill herself tonight!"

You see, sometimes Pop got the idea that Kossan's mother was going to gas herself to death. This is the way it happened: he'd look out the window and see Kossan jumping rope. (By the way, she was a champion rope-jumper, rhythmic and daring, like a pro boxer at the top of his form.) And then Pop, who'd probably had a drop or two to drink, would remember how his sister Astrid had sent her kid out into the yard before she turned on the burners. So then Mom would send me up to borrow a cup of sugar or coffee to make sure that it was only in Poppa's imagination. They didn't really need to send me, though. All they really had to do was check to see if the door was sealed with tape—that was the surest sign.

Gas and mushrooms—those were things that scared Pop. Gas exploded and sent arms and legs flying in all directions. "Like this!" he'd say, and he'd throw out his arms so violently that they'd almost fly out of their sockets. Mushrooms were poisonous. You'd writhe in terrible agony before you died, and you'd plead and beg the people around you to finish you off with a stab of the knife or another portion of mushrooms.

"But why would she want to kill herself?" Mom would wonder out loud. "She doesn't have to worry. No husband's bugging her!"

What she meant was that when Pop had a little too much, his jealousy would get to him; Mom was good-looking with her brown eyes and long black hair. And then there'd be quarreling and fighting that could be heard through the whole backhouse. The day after, everything would go back to usual; Mom would be humming and cleaning and cooking, and Pop would come home from the factory all sober and bursting with energy—he'd repair the plumbing, put up a shelf, cut my hair. But actually his jealousy had some foundation: as a young girl Mom *had* known a boy from a high-class family. He'd become a civil engineer, and she still exchanged letters with him from time to time.

"He thinks I've come up in the world because I live in Ostermalm," she'd laugh. But his letters didn't even come to our house; I had to go to the post office and pick them up at General Delivery so that the ladies in the backhouse wouldn't gossip.

"How come your father fights with your mother?" Kossan asked me one time.

I told her it was the same way with Olle and Sixten's parents, and all the others too. Sixten even got whipped whenever his father felt like it. "It's going to be great when I get to America," he'd say. "They don't beat kids there."

"Your Mom just turned on the light," I said to Kossan.

"Then she's awake. She's got the night shift. I better go."

She stood up. I was sitting—or reclining, actually—on the top step. The air was balmy, a real Indian summer evening. She went over to the carpet rack to get her tennis balls. Then something curious happened right before my eyes. All the houses seemed to fade away: the oak became a live, comforting being, and somewhere I could hear a river gurgling. It was another time, another place. And Kossan became a silvery, diaphanous figure who floated across glorious, eternal fields of Paradise.

"Drink to live."

I regretted those words.

When I looked at her standing by the carpet rack, I remembered a day in early spring when Max and I were throwing darts at the target he'd set up in the yard. Kossan was running around with the little kids, and suddenly she popped up behind the target. At the same time one of us—I can't for the life of me remember who—threw a dart that missed the target by a mile. It went straight for her face, for her eye.

We rushed over, petrified with fear. The dart had got her just above the eyebrow, a red dot which soon filled with blood. She gave the dart back to us. "Ah, that was nothing. Just an accident, nothing to worry about." Her calm and patience really touched me; I felt like she was our mother and we were two small boys.

"Kossan!" I cried.

She turned around by the door. I wanted to tell her some of what I was feeling, but I couldn't make a sound. Finally I waved at her. After a few seconds she waved back and went inside.

15

In *Ivanhoe* the group jousts were considered more dangerous than the individual ones, but in Buffalo Bill's tournament it was the other way around. Only the best kids dared to go up against the Black Knight, for if they didn't manage to hold their own, they'd get booed and made fun of mercilessly by the preppies. In the turmoil of a group fight, however, people didn't notice so much if you held your lance awkwardly or didn't know how to handle your horse.

That was what made Max feel a little better. He knew he wasn't much of a fighter, and he really didn't want to be in the tournament anyway. Nobody expected great things of him; if he could just parry a few thrusts before he got knocked off, he'd have done his part. "Holding the bets pays more than fighting," he muttered to me.

"Not if the Nameless Knights win," I pointed out. "Have you worked out some kind of plan?"

"Plan? Sure. I'm going to follow Ernst's advice: 'Rush out and knock 'em all down!' How's that for a plan?"

In school it didn't make any difference that I was just a horse for a Nameless Knight. We horses were envied and admired just because we were in the preppies' tournament. Kids asked us what we thought of Henning's chances against the Black Knight, and they listened to our answers as respectfully as the preppies listened to Henning's.

The day of the tournament was warm and sunny, a cloudless day precisely like the one in *Ivanhoe* when the real tournament took place, the one in which the Black Knight intervened on Ivanhoe's behalf. As soon as I got home from school I wandered around the yard restlessly, surprised that Kossan was calmly playing with the little kids. I'd told her that she wouldn't make her entrance before it was time for the big battle with the Black Knight.

"If you want to see me and Max fight, you can watch through the keyhole," I said, "while Henning puts on his costume."

At long last, Henning and Max came downstairs. Carefully, Henning spread his gold tunic with the red collar over my bough—though, naturally, he didn't know it was mine. He stuck the point of the lance into the ground and hung the gold helmet on the other end; it looked fabulous. Then he sat down in his place by the trunk of the tree with a German grammar book in his hand; the main attraction of the tournament looked totally unconcerned about the coming battle.

Max, wearing a light-brown tunic (the Nameless Knights could wear any colors they wanted), was nervous. What would happen if he got hit in the head and got a concussion? Or if he fell off his horse and broke his leg? He kept taking out his Omega, opening it, looking and sighing; he wanted it to be over as fast as possible.

"Get going!" Henning said finally. "Kossan and I will come later. We've got plenty of time."

Buffalo Bill's neighborhood wasn't especially far from our domain. The last time we'd gone into his yard through the main entrance off the wide thoroughfare which led to the large raised yard. This time, however, we followed the narrow parallel street, Maiden Street, till we came to a beat-up outer door which opened into a dark vestibule. Up a half-stairway was a wide landing with a wooden door painted brown; behind it Nils-Wilhelm had prepared himself for his entrance, and this was the same place which Henning would use to put on his golden outfit and get up on Kossan. We pushed the door open and came out next to the stairway that led to the upper yard.

"See you!" said Max dejectedly, and with his lance dragging behind him he vanished behind the white curtain in front of the stairway. The stairs were already crowded with little kids; they looked expectantly at Max and me and whispered to each other. I was almost blinded by the harsh afternoon light which filled the arena and reflected off the white wall where the spectators were gathered.

A shrill whistle pierced the air. It came from Olle in the horses' corral. I squinted out over the battle area; it was bigger than I'd thought. To my right Buffalo Bill was piling up his cork cones; behind him the Boy Scout was busy trying to get his blue and gold crate to stand straight. In front of the corral was a sign in block letters: KEEP OUT! ONLY FOR HORSES! KEEP OUT!

"You're late. I was beginning to think that Max had backed out," said Olle. "If he had, you'd really have missed out on something. Buffalo Bill was just here, and he says that the place is packed three-deep. They're probably going to be extra generous today because they just got their allowances."

Sixteen was throwing knives with two other guys. Some were playing tic-tac-toe on the ground, while others lay stretched out on their backs talking. I squatted next to Olle by the wall and glanced up. It hadn't looked so high last time when I'd been up there and looked down. But now! God, the idea of falling off! No wonder everyone thought that Henning was brave to sit there and dangle his legs—not to mention when he stood on the edge to deliver his challenge to the Black Knight.

From down here it felt like being in an abyss. Like Jack London had felt, even though he had only been a temporary "guest" there. He'd dressed up like a bum and been accepted into the city's worst slums. But when two real bums had found out that he was really a fine gentleman, they'd become completely confused, silent, and self-conscious. For them, Jack London was a creature from a totally foreign world. It was in just the same way that I'd been taken for a preppie until Rebecca exposed me. *À outrance*—with bare weapons, a fight to the death! The preppie who'd turned to me had been so uncomfortable and nervous when he'd realized that the person behind him was a kid from public school! So now I was back in the abyss with my own kind. When I thought of the others, the preppies, standing above me, I felt a pang of longing.

If I stayed down here in the abyss, the Stockholm Monster would strangle me. I had to outsmart him, but how? By saving money and studying the way Kossan planned to? Should I let the Monster suck the marrow out of Olle and Sigge and the others? But that's just what a preppie like Jack London had complained about: that people didn't care enough about each other's suffering. What had he written? I wished I had Kossan's good memory. Something about a race of greedy two-legged beings who stood between the worker and his pay, who exploited the poor and the ignorant. Maybe I had no right to think just of myself. If I joined with Olle and Sigge and the others in the abyss, could we defeat the Monster together?

The brilliant, piercing sound of the bugle came as suddenly and surprisingly as the last time. It had

an almost magical influence on us; we leapt up and
massed expectantly at the foot of the white wall.
Everybody peered up towards the top of the wall.
Blue sky and crowds of faces, most of them brown
and sunburned. As though cutting its way through a
fog, Buffalo Bill's voice welcomed everyone to the
tournament. Then came the words we were waiting
for:

"*Largesse, largesse,* honorable gentlemen and
beautiful ladies!"

A forest of arms and white hands above us that
looked like a blossom opening and closing. Money
came flying down from the skies! Money, money!
And at that very moment something happened inside
me: greed took me over. I became totally crazed. I
had to have money no matter what, money was
everything. I didn't even recognize myself; gone
were all thoughts of working together, of comrade-
ship.

Pushing and hitting the others, I got wildly angry
as a boy grabbed a coin from right under my nose. I
knocked over Olle to get at another that was rolling
away; he whirled around but when he saw who it
was, he grinned a devilish grin with bared teeth as if
to say, "Well done, Roland my boy, but next time it's
my turn!" All of us ran around like madmen, tripping
each other, kicking and scratching and digging our
hands into the ground. I got hit so hard from a flying
foot right across my face that I thought I was going
to get a bloody nose, and a sharp elbow hit me in the

chest and I almost blacked out. But I didn't give up. Money! Money from the skies! It boomed in my ears. I had the strength of a giant, I could fight for money forever.

But then it stopped. What had happened?

And then I knew: it was over. Olle was rubbing a sore knee, Sigge stood counting his money like everyone else. Everybody was occupied with himself. Only slowly, as though from a distance, the sounds of the outer world started to filter back: the murmur of the preppies on the wall, Buffalo Bill's voice as he read the rules of the tournament, the jabber of the little kids. I'd squeezed my money so tightly that the coins were slick with sweat; I finally dropped them into my pants pocket. I could count them later; right now it felt delicious to float suspended in uncertainty about how much I'd managed to grab.

Above us the cheering began. The knights had entered from the space under the stairway and walked towards Buffalo Bill in the middle of the arena. In comparison to the Grand Street Knights all dressed in blue, the Nameless Knights were a ragged bunch. Max came last. With his lance in his hand and his helmet on his head, at least he didn't look *completely* harmless. Buffalo Bill made a sign to us horses, and we trudged obediently towards him.

One after another, the knights climbed up on their horses and received their lances. While I waited for my turn, I realized that maybe the preppies would recognize me: Roland, the phony preppie. But it didn't matter any longer. I'd never be a part of them again.

Max and I were the last pair.

"Yea, Max!" shrieked several preppies encouragingly as he climbed up on my back. I clasped my hands across my stomach to make sure I had a firm grip. Buffalo Bill gave him the lance with the cork cone fixed to its end. I hurried after the other four Nameless Knights; they all stood right behind. the line in front of the stairway, and I found a position farthest over to the right.

On the opposite side of the arena the Grand Street Knights gathered in an unbroken blue line. From the Karla Street Knights they'd learned to raise their lances simultaneously and cry: "For the honor of Grand Street!"

But Max whispered, "Don't be in such a hurry!"

I realized that I was shuffling nervously in place. My hands were very sweaty, and Max felt heavier than usual.

"Laissez aller!"

Buffalo Bill's shout was followed by the signal to charge, this time a provocatively short, almost biting bugle blast. The Grand Street Knights lowered their lances and came thundering towards us. Frankly, it was very frightening and overwhelming. It was only when we too got going that I even noticed that Sixten was farthest out on their left flank; somehow that comforted me, and instantly Max became as light as a knapsack again.

I ran eagerly towards Sixten. As we neared each other I moved so that Max, who was left-handed, would be able to fight from the left side. When he suddenly found us on the wrong side, the Grand Street Knight got confused, and his thrust had no power behind it. Sixten and I stared for several seconds into each other's eyes. We both saw and didn't see each other—our usual friendship was gone. I whirled around with Max and followed Sixten's feet with my eyes; it was like a dance, we retreated, advanced, sidestepped. I was happily surprised that Max hadn't fallen off yet; perhaps Sixten's Grand Street Knight wasn't much of a fighter either.

The whole experience was confusing. The world had shrunk. Dimly, like the rumble of a thunderstorm or the roar of traffic, the cries of disappointment and the memory of the bugle's high-pitched notes worked their way through to me. Around me the knights grunted, moaned, screamed disconnectedly. "Get him, Klaus! Thrust, thrust! Be careful! Watch your flank!"

When a knight or a horse fell, gravel and sand rose like a cloud. Sixten disappeared, Olle appeared in his place. He rushed at me like an animal, his face right against mine, his eyes glowing like a madman's. We butted each other; above our heads the knights' lances clashed. Another horse pushed between us, and we were thrown apart.

One of the Grand Street Knights came at Max furiously. I caught a glimpse of his blue tunic over the horse's blond mane. As Max parried, the lances clattered dryly, and Max was forced to lean backwards, forcing me to back up. The enemy horse made a quick, sidestepping movement, not giving Max enough time to change grips on his lance; he was hit by a powerful thrust that I could feel in my arms and legs.

"Ow!" he cried, the lance falling out of his hand. Trying vainly to keep from falling, he grabbed my shirt and almost tore it off as he slipped off my back and landed on the ground with a thud. Tears of disappointment and anger filled my eyes.

Max struggled to his feet. I stood alone, relieved of the burden on my back, and looked all around. Amazed, I saw that there were three Nameless Knights left and only two Grand Streeters. I hadn't had any idea how the rest of the battle had gone— Sixten's sneakers and Olle's forelock were about all that I'd seen. The two Grand Street Knights were quickly outmaneuvered by the three Nameless Knights and knocked off their horses; the preppies applauded, cheered and booed. The Grand Street fans were almost beside themselves: nobody thought the Nameless Knights had had a chance of winning, and now they were a big sensation.

"Damn it! We lost again! But we'll get even next week!" said Olle as he spit out gravel and grass. Sixten joined us, and we walked over to the water faucet next to the tin cellar door. We struggled with the other horses to get a drink and splash water on our sweaty foreheads; the water was ice-cold.

"Come on, Olle. Let's go," said Sixten.

"Aren't you staying to see the Black Knight and Henning?"

"Naw, I've got to get home and help Dad. One beating for the day is enough, thank you. And Olle's got another money-making scheme."

They—and most of the other horses—disappeared. Only three of us were left, and we drifted back to the stairway where we sat on the ground below the little kids. When Max came out, I saw that he'd changed clothes; he lit up when he saw me.

"It was easier than I thought," he said. "But now I've got to go and take care of the betting. There aren't many kids who are going to bet on the Black Knight today. Get out of the way, kids. I'm coming through!"

16

This time it was the Black Knight's turn to come in first.

"Who do you think he is?" I asked Pelle, a stocky boy with a deep voice who went to my school; he'd been a horse for a Nameless Knight, too.

"The Black Knight? How come you don't know? He's one of us! That's why I hope he knocks that Henning right on his ass!"

One of us! Wouldn't it have been great if Pelle wasn't just being sarcastic! Everybody took it for granted that he was a preppie, or at the very least one of their mortal enemies from North Latin. If the Black Knight was an ordinary kid from public school, it would have explained why he wore a mask—so that he could get into the tournament. Maybe he did come from the Deepest Darkness, from poverty's deep despair and degradation, and far, far from rich peoples' hopes and resources. Maybe he really was a worker's son who was better than the preppies in every way! Maybe he could teach all of us!

"He plays in a real jazz combo," said Pelle.

"The Black Knight?"

"Idiot. The bugle player. He's in Kiddla Kiddie's band."

That impressed him more than the fact that the bugler was a Boy Scout!

Behind the bugler I saw that there was new graffiti chalked on the brick wall.

"The Black Knight = Devil." "What's going on in Russia?" "Buffalo Bill is a shit." Just as I read the last one and felt a little shocked, Buffalo Bill came down the staircase; the intermission was over. He saw what I was looking at and laughed good-naturedly.

"That's okay. It's good publicity. All I care about is that people know my name."

The cork cones had already been put back next to the two doors, and the Scout stood ready on the blue and gold box by the brick wall. He held the bugle a few inches from his lips. It grew completely quiet. Then Buffalo Bill came out into the arena and raised his arm.

"Honorable gentlemen and beautiful ladies! Now comes the battle we've all been waiting for! The Black Knight from the Deepest Darkness will meet Henning, a knight of noble birth. As everyone knows, Henning is descended from a brilliant and illustrious line of knights famed in Swedish history. I am sure it is going to be an exciting match between these two

118

courageous knights, but whatever the outcome I ask you to pay a nice tribute to the Black Knight for his previous victories by giving him a round of applause. May the best man win!"

He went over to the cellar door. His black cape fluttered around his legs, but he moved deliberately and with dignity. The latch of the cellar door dropped; one of us had forgotten to close it properly. Buffalo Bill turned the large key in the lock, and the bugle sounded with short, military crispness; the bugler almost made it sound like a complaint, as though he'd only signal the Black Knight's entrance unwillingly.

The door was flung open, and the dreaded black phantom appeared again on the Mute's back. From my perspective he looked even more frightening than before. The Mute stood broad-legged, solid, merged with the black figure who sat deadly still as Buffalo Bill fastened the cone to the glistening lance. Behind them, the doorway was a black hole; it looked as though they had emerged from out of the under-world, ready to take over a world which was about to turn pale, shrivel and die. Something ominous surrounded them: the applause from the preppies was hesitant, short, half-hearted.

Buffalo Bill crossed the arena and stood close to us. When he picked up another cone, he turned again to the field of combat and the bugle sounded, this time with a more festive, golden brightness . . . or was it just my imagination?

As Buffalo Bill opened the door, there was a sigh, a murmur of expectation from the rows of spectators on the edge of the wall. I wondered what they'd think of Henning in his golden armor; he was sure to outdo Nils-Wilhelm.

Henning entered on Kossan's back!

My heart swelled with pride. Henning and Kossan from my yard! Of course they'd win! He looked magnificent as he sat straight and serious in his tight gold costume with its red collar, golden lance, and gold helmet with a sharply cut trim from forehead to neck to make it look less like a hat.

Buffalo Bill looked at Kossan, hesitated a moment, and then fastened the cork cone to the end of the lance. Kossan stood still with her drab red head slightly bowed. A strange, hissing murmur rose from the audience, a surprised buzzing and whispering that grew in strength until it seemed like it would build into an explosion. Suddenly someone up on the wall shouted in a clear and distinct voice that could be heard throughout the whole arena:

"It's Kossan! Henning's horse is Kossan! A girl!"

Delightedly the little kids on the stairway repeated the cry.

"Kossan! The horse is named Kossan! Kossan!"

The name sounded comic in their happy, childish voices. The preppies laughed, first at the little kids, then at their own people who shrieked with an edge of malice and contempt in their voices.

"Henning on Kossan! The Knight of the Mournful Countenance!"

120

"No, you mean the Knight *on* the Mournful Countenance!"

It seemed as if there were a lot of them who were envious of Henning. Now they saw a way to get back at him safely and anonymously, as just voices in the crowd.

"Henning! Have you milked her yet?"

"Kossan! Show him where your udders are!"

"Henning! Does this make you a cowboy?"

After every line, the laughter grew, finally building into a huge, derisive evil wave of laughter that rolled out over the yard. With each new joke it became even more angry and raw, as though howling spirits and demons had come up with the Black Knight from the underworld.

"Henning, what breed of cow is that?"

"Must be a half-breed!"

"It's a freak-breed, that's what it is!"

"Moo, moo, moo," someone suddenly bellowed very convincingly. Immediately everybody including the little kids started doing it. It became a deafening lowing sound, like the mooing of a thousand cows.

"Moo . . . moo . . . moo!"

In the middle of the commotion, Buffalo Bill decided to continue.

"*Laissez aller!*" he shouted. The bugle cut through the din for a few short seconds, but then the lowing, booing, and coarse jeering grew more intense again.

"Why doesn't she move?"

"She's probably having a calf!"

"Or dropping a turd!"

The Black Knight started towards them, but Kossan stood still, paralyzed. Henning slapped her on her shoulder, and finally she took a few painful, arduous steps out into the arena as though she had a giant on her back; the incessant mooing seemed like an invisible wall she couldn't break through. The Black Knight was already close. Henning lowered his lance but the Mute maneuvered quickly around Kossan who turned as though she weighed a ton.

Everything that they did met with extra booing and evil cackling; Henning squirmed and twisted on Kossan's back, but she could hardly move.

"Put them out of their misery!" someone cried.

In the same instant came the *coup de grace* from an angle in front that didn't allow Henning any time to parry. The thrust didn't look particularly powerful, but Henning was thrown backwards and he fell to the ground; Kossan stood there alone, her head bent.

His blond hair tousled, his helmet on the ground, Henning got up slowly, his face chalk white with anger in spite of his suntan. His eyes were hard blue diamonds, his mouth a narrow line; this catastrophe would cost him the leadership of the preppies. His enemies wouldn't let him forget for a moment that now he was Henning the Buffoon; Henning Who Rode the Cow and Fell in the Shit; Henning, the Total Fake!

"Now who's the hotshot, Army brat?" shrieked someone bitterly.

"Now the general's going to be taken down a peg!"

122

Suddenly Henning picked up his lance from the ground. He was so upset and furious he was shaking. He raised the javelin and took a pair of long strides towards the Black Knight. The lowing and guffaws died down a little. Henning tore off the cork cone and threw it aside, then raised the lance with the sharp point towards the Black Knight and bellowed over all the mooing and laughter:

"Black Knight! I challenge you to a battle *à outrance!*"

À outrance—with bare weapons, a fight to the death.

It was quiet as death.

Totally quiet. I wouldn't have believed that there could be such a silence with so many people around.

The Black Knight sat motionless, as if in thought. Everyone waited breathlessly. Then he pulled the cone off with a smooth motion so that the needle-sharp metal point was laid bare and swung the lance defiantly in Henning's direction, still without uttering a word.

"A outrance!" shouted Henning, and he lifted his lance.

The Black Knight nodded and saluted him with the bare point of his lance. A second later the Mute turned on his heels and vanished with his rider into the darkness of the cellar. Buffalo Bill closed the door again and quickly turned the key in the lock, as though he were afraid that if he didn't they'd start fighting each other right away.

Henning went back to Kossan in complete silence. Then somebody started clapping.

A few seconds later all the preppies were clapping, a sound like the drumming of heavy rain. They were applauding! An applause that grew and grew as the lowing and laughter had earlier—and it grew to an intense, powerful hurricane of applause that seemed as though it would never stop.

With his new-found defiance Henning had again proven that he was the bravest of the preppies; he'd gotten back his position as leader. But he didn't seem even to hear the applause as he passed by us with a stony expression on his pale face. Nudging her, he kept the embarrassed Kossan in front of him, and they ducked through the wooden door which led to Maiden Street and out of our sight.

17

If only Kossan had been a real horse!

We loved horses. We even had friends who couldn't read *The Death of Jumper* because they couldn't stand that Texas Jack's horse died. And Kossan didn't like books like that very much either.

"Now if they wrote something about *Texas Jack*'s death, I'd read it in a shot. It would serve him right. He's a real Jonas Fjeld type!"

And at the movies we didn't care very much about the actors. Tom Mix, Buck Jones, Ken Maynard— they were all pretty much the same to us. But their horses! We argued about which one was the most beautiful, and we thought they were the smartest animals in the world.

"The horse is not a terribly intelligent beast, but it does have an excellent memory," Henning would say as if he knew everything there was to be known.

My favorite was called Tarzan. It was a strange

name for a horse but not really any stranger than calling a human Kossan. Tarzan was a palomino, and he was even smarter than his master. He bowed politely, lay down and played dead, pulled Ken Maynard out of the river, bit through rope and saved Ken whenever the bad guys captured him. In every film he rushed into burning buildings and saved the heroine, and in the last scene he'd nudge the shy and slightly awkward Ken right into the girl's arms. Even though he was a horse, he was human too.

If only Kossan had been a horse like that! Instead she'd stood there like a dumb cow, humiliating Henning and our yard. I was so angry that I could have screamed. Not even the thought of the money I'd gotten, which would bring me closer to my "O" model Erector set, could soothe my rage.

"Heard your Henning really blew it," said Olle the next day in school.

"It was Kossan's fault. And she was so good in practice!"

"That's what you get for depending on girls. What really happened, though? Did she get cold feet?"

"I don't know. She got completely paralyzed just because they laughed at her. But Henning'll get his revenge, you can be sure of that. He's going to fight with bare weapons!"

"Bare weapons! Well, but they're going to have big shields; otherwise Buffalo Bill can't let them fight. Shields like in *Ivanhoe*—that's what the preppies in my yard said last night. And they'll only be allowed to aim for the shields so that it'll be almost like with the cork cones. If they didn't, they could really kill each other, you idiot. Although everybody would probably love to see if Henning's blood really is blue!"

Shields. Of course. I hadn't thought about how they'd work it out, even though I knew my *Ivanhoe.* In the book the knights had huge shields, and their opponents would lower their lances and try to knock them off their horses with a direct hit.

After school I made a little tour of Ostermalm Square. Eventually when I got back to our yard, I saw Kossan sitting by the carpet rack with the little kids around her as if nothing had happened. That bothered me, and the timid look she gave me when she saw me coming made me even angrier. She looked so damn guilty, the way she glanced quickly up at me and then down again to the jump rope she was threading through the handles.

"It was all your fault!" I screamed with righteous indignation. "You just stood there like a cow! Henning would have won! Now you made him fight the Black Knight with bare weapons! It's all your fault!"

She bowed her head towards the rope. The little kids moved aside a little fearfully while I raved on. (It felt really good to put her down.)

"Why did you do it? You looked completely crazy! You just stood there gaping like a bowl of Jello!"

"I know. I know it was my fault," she mumbled.

"But why? Why? Max and I did great. We weren't

a bit nervous. You were just scared of the Mute, right?"

She shook her head.

"It just happened," she said almost inaudibly.

"It just happened!" I mimicked sardonically. "So who's supposed to be Henning's horse now?"

"Me."

"What do you mean, 'me'?"

"I'm going to be Henning's horse again."

"You? But how can you be his horse when you messed up so badly? When did he tell you?"

"Yesterday. After . . . afterwards. And this time it'll be all right. Max took my measurements. Henning and I will beat the Black Knight this time."

She was still holding her head bowed—all her attention was on the rope, but in her voice was the same single-minded determination that she had when she played boxball, that toughness and tenacity that made her fight to the very end.

"Henning took measurements? Of what?"

"They're going to put something on me so that no one will recognize me. . . . Okay, I fixed the rope, Stina. Come on, we'll play follow-the-leader."

Suddenly she ran away with the little kids fluttering at her heels. Of course, I thought to myself. He's a genius. If they put a disguise on Kossan, she'll be as anonymous as the Black Knight. Nobody will know that it's she. Maybe they'll suspect, but they won't know for sure. It'll be the same way they suspect the Black Knight is Uno or Carl Magnus or a kid from North Latin—no one knows for sure!

A moment later Henning and Max came down into the yard. As usual, they were bareheaded. But if we played boxball on the sidewalk in front of the house, they'd have to run back to get their caps. A teacher of theirs might come by and they'd get a demerit just for not having their caps on.

Max was carrying a bundle of brown material over his arm. He said with pride in his voice:

"I could have beaten Ossian if I'd had time to get my lance in a good position."

"Where's Kossan?" said Henning, who couldn't find her in the flock of kids.

"Kossan!" I shouted. She looked up from the cellar stairway and came hesitantly towards us. Henning looked her over sharply and then surveyed the yard.

"We can't stay here," he decided. "Too many inquisitive eyes. We'll go over to the outhouses."

"What are we going to do?" I asked.

"We're going to change Kossan into a battle horse," answered Max eagerly.

18

Furthest back in the right-hand corner of the yard where most of the time wash was hanging out to dry was the old-fashioned outhouse above the washroom. The backhouse had been modernized to the extent that a few years earlier, they'd put in tiny toilet rooms in the building. Our w.c. was so small that you could hardly turn around once you were inside ("If you get an erection when you're sitting down," Poppa would say, "you push the door open.") And yet we thought it was the most luxurious thing in the world not to have an outhouse—something which only Olle objected to strongly.

"If all this modernizing keeps up, my Dad will be out of a job."

From the narrow sides of the rectangular washroom, stairs led up to a walkway between the two rows of toilets. They'd taken out the seats and everything, but they'd left the slatted doors in place. In several of the stalls there was a lot of junk, but otherwise they were empty, just like the section with the urinals—or piss-house, as Pop more accurately called it. You could be totally undisturbed in the place; no grownups ever came in anymore because there was still a smell, a weak yet acrid stench. In spite of warnings that the whole place would burn up if we weren't careful, sometimes we'd gather around a candle in the winter darkness.

"We've made a horse covering for Kossan," Max explained. "It was really fun to cut it and pin it up. Maybe I'll be a tailor instead of a banker! Okay, Kossan, let's try it!"

He untied his bundle. Even I could see that it was expensive material, thick, dark-brown cloth that he'd gotten from "one of the rolls."

"Poppa gets them from a wholesaler in place of the interest on a loan. We have piles of them just lying in the closet getting moth-eaten."

Henning put Kossan on the wooden walkway in front of stall No. 7. All his actions were marked by calm, collected determination, and yet, even though he was right there and intensely involved in what he was doing, I had the feeling that he was also somewhere else. On what distant battlefield was he fighting his battles? For once a phrase from one of my books occurred to me, to *me* who could never remember a single quote: "He was older than the days he'd seen and the breaths he'd drawn. He was a link between the past and the present."

In the middle of a big piece of cloth Max had made a hole which he placed over Kossan's head. The cloth

131

fell around her like a poncho. He'd cut out four rectangular pieces which he wound around Kossan's bare arms and legs, and then fastened them with safety pins. I helped too.

"This is just temporary," Max said. "I'm going to sew them up so they'll be like pipes Kossan can pull onto her arms and legs."

Kossan—all covered in brown now—fingered the cloth.

"Such fine material," she said.

"Put the horse head on her," Henning said.

It was only then that I noticed the big bundle had a horse's head in it too. It was the most artful mask I'd ever seen; made from stiff cardboard (or some kind of stuff like it), it was shaped like a real horse's nose, only perhaps slightly shorter and more blunt. Brown cloth was fastened to the lower edge of the head, and when Kossan got it on, the cloth fell over her shoulders. On the sides of the nose were holes for Kossan's eyes, and two pointy ears had been fastened to the sides of the head. The nose was open at the bottom and you could get a glimpse of Kossan's mouth and chin, but that didn't really matter, Max said. Everyone would see her from above.

"It's tight, but that's the way it should be," he explained. "Henning made it that way. Turn around, Kossan!"

Slowly she turned around and faced us. We were stunned. The horse head completely transformed her. Was Kossan really standing in front of us? This brown horse who now ran back and forth shaking its

132

long head? The faint smell of toilets reminded me of stables and made the illusion even stronger.

"Damn, all she needs is a feedbag!" Max said finally. "Can you see anything in there?"

"Not much," came the muffled voice in the horse head.

"What do you think, Henning?" Max looked questioningly at him. Henning nodded and rummaged through the bundle which Max had put on the wooden floor.

"But she can't see!" I said.

"I know," he answered curtly.

He took out a pair of thin leather bridles. They were fastened to a kind of bit, a short, narrow, rubberlike rod which had round pieces with rings at both ends. He reached the bit in under the horse head and placed it in Kossan's mouth. Max and I crouched and looked up. Kossan had the bit in her mouth and the rings in the corners of her lips—like a real horse. Her lips were moving, she was searching for the best place to put her tongue. Henning pulled the reins over her head and let them rest on her neck.

He led Kossan over to the stairs, went up to the next-to-last step and climbed onto her slightly bent back. Taking the reins in his left hand, he clicked his tongue and she took a few steps towards the yard. But when he pulled the left rein she pulled her head to the left:

"Not like that, not like that!" he yelled impatiently. "*All* of you has to turn!"

"But I can't see anything!" she protested.

"You don't have to! Follow the bridle! How else can I maneuver you! When we're actually in the arena it's going to be so noisy you won't be able to hear a word. Nils-Wilhelm gave orders to his horse to turn, but he couldn't hear him!"

"Then what about the Black Knight and the Mute?" Max said.

"That's different. The Mute is trained. They've probably worked out a system where he steers him with little movements of his knees."

With Henning on her back Kossan circled the small area in front of the washroom where the laundry was usually hung. Little by little they improved: Kossan learned to stop when Henning pulled in the reins, to rush forward when he let go of them, to turn completely when he pulled hard on one rein. It was weird to see how quickly they learned to do things without saying a single word.

"We've got to train more," Henning said when he slid off. Kossan stood stock still. Henning took out the bit and dried it on his pants. "Take off her stuff."

When we took off the horse head, she shook her head; we were almost relieved to find our old Kossan was still there.

"How does it feel?" Max said.

"Hot. Just like being a horse. It hurts my mouth a little, but not all that much."

"She'll get used to it," Henning said. "All horses do."

"It'll be even warmer and heavier for you when

Henning gets his shield and lance and mask. What equipment! Not even Ivanhoe would have a chance!"

A whole horde of little kids came running, and they surrounded Kossan.

"Kossan, Kossan, where have you been? Stina's rope broke again!"

She ran off with them into the yard. Max collected all the things; he suggested that they keep them in the stalls which used to belong to the seventh floor. Henning looked towards Kossan.

"Well, she's no Tony," he said, "but she'll do."

Tony, that was Tom Mix's horse. Max had told me that Tom Mix was the only movie hero Henning liked. Perhaps it was because Tom Mix was a perfect Boy Scout: straight, brave, patriotic.

19

"You really looked like a horse today," I was saying to Kossan. "Don't worry about being laughed at this time. You looked at least as scary as the Mute."

We were sitting in the darkness curled up by the carpet rack. It was almost time for us to go up for the night. After both the preppies had gone up, we'd rummaged around in the outhouse and found a pair of stilts in the rubbish. We'd taken turns walking around the yard with them, trying to see who could take the biggest steps. At one point Mom had walked by and said, "Don't break your necks, kids."

"We should tell Buffalo Bill," said Kossan, "to have a stilt competition."

The only light in the yard came from the back-house, from an apartment with a light in the kitchen or bedroom, a few bright rectangles on the ground. Sometimes when I was alone in the evening I would climb up into the oak, but there really wasn't anything special to see—just Poppa puttering around in his short nightshirt (which was really just a wornout everyday shirt). In the front house all the shades were drawn; these were the windows I was interested in. With a little luck you might see one of the maids undressing or even necking with a sailor on a Saturday evening before she remembered to pull down the shade.

"You trotted around with Henning on your back as if you'd been doing it your whole life," I said. "So what made you stand like a tree when the Black Knight came towards you? Don't you remember that Henning said that the attack was the most important thing? Did you get scared because everybody was watching? Because they laughed at you?"

"Not at all."

"So why then? Because it just happened?"

"I know why," she answered in a low voice with her face turned away; she was pretending to look up at her own dark kitchen window.

"Why?"

"I don't want to say."

I realized that pushing her wouldn't help. Once a few years ago I'd tried to force her to tell me which of the little kids dropped a waterbag from the stairway window right on my head. I'd twisted her arm and tortured her, but all she'd said was, "No, I won't say a thing. Find out for yourself!"

"You don't like Henning," I said.

"I do and I don't." She fell silent, but when I didn't say anything she went on as if encouraged by my silence. "Do you remember last spring when all four of us were playing boxball? When he told me to read *The Call of the Wild*?"

I nodded.

It had been an early summer evening just before school ended and Henning and Max went with their families to the islands out in the archipelago. We'd drawn boxes on the sidewalk in front of the house where the ball bounced better than in the yard. As we were getting ready to start, Kossan came home from the library. Out of the goodness of our hearts we said that she could be the fourth man; she and Henning would be one team and Max and I the other—Henning of course was the best player among us. It soon became clear, however, that she was so good—I knew this already—that she and Henning, to his great pleasure, won every game.

Afterwards, we crossed the empty street in the gathering dusk and climbed up on the window ledge of the cigar store just opposite our building. As usual, I wanted to know which books Kossan had taken out. One was *The Brown Palace* and the other *The People of the Abyss* by Jack London, a favorite book of hers which she'd borrowed before. Henning just sniffed at *The People of the Abyss*:

"Jack London wrote only one good book," he said. *"The Call of the Wild."*

Suddenly he became—for him—very talkative and enthusiastic. He told us all about Buck, how no dog could equal his lightning-quick reflexes, his strength, his cleverness: he survived because he was the strongest of them all.

"It has been shown scientifically," Henning said, "that only the strong survive. Winners produce other winners, and that way you can create a chosen race that is strong, intelligent, superior in every way. In the book, Buck becomes the father of a whole race of perfect wolf dogs!"

"Let's hope that they stay in Alaska," said Max. "I don't want to get torn apart by one of those Hounds of the Baskervilles or whatever the hell they are."

"Beings like Buck, Jonas Fjeld and Wolf Larsen in *The Sea Wolf*, they're above the rules of ordinary people because they're better and stronger than anybody else! *The Call of the Wild!* You should read it!" he said, turning to Kossan whose face turned burning red. She nodded: Right, I've got to read it someday.

"So did you read it?" I asked her now as we stood by the carpet rack.

"I couldn't borrow it from school until we began at the end of August," she said. "It was a real old copy, you know, the one with the nice St. Bernard on the cover."

"Yeah, it's so old it says, 'By *Mr*. Jack London.'"

"When I read it I saw Henning instead of Buck in front of me the whole time. Henning was the one fighting with Spitz. Henning was the one who controlled the wolves and became their leader. It was as if Jack London had written a book about Henning himself—or at least someone like him."

The simplicity and quiet melancholy in her voice impressed me.

"Oh, sure," I said. "And I bet you're that old trapper Thornton. The one who took care of Henning the dog. And when you got killed by the Indians, Henning came running and howled on your grave. *The Call of Ostermalm,* right?"

I couldn't shut myself up. By making fun of her and making it all into a big joke I took the sting out of her seriousness and defended against the feelings of friendship which we might have felt. I couldn't stand how big and ugly she was with that dull red hair and those disgusting freckles.

For a while she didn't say anything; it was as if she wanted to let my words just evaporate. Finally she continued.

"It was Henning, not Buck, who threw himself at the Indians' throats, who chased them and knocked them down on the ground like deer. And I don't like *that* Henning at all. Didn't you notice how quiet Max got that night? Why do some people think they're better than other people just because the others aren't as rich, as strong, or come from a different race?

"Maybe somebody at home tells them they're better."

And I almost added: at my house Mom and Pop think we're better than your unmarried mother and her bastard child. But instead I said, "So how come then you're going to be his horse? I don't hear you complaining about that!"

"I don't know. All the girls say that he's the handsomest boy in all of Ostermalm."

140

"Mom says that too. The general's handsome boy. Maybe you're in love with him."

"I know somebody who is," she said. "Rebecca. She's crazy about him. Everybody knows it. She does everything she can to get him interested. But he doesn't care at all about her. I don't like that Wolf Henning, but I can understand her—it's funny, but when I *look* at him I get all confused. My head stops working. I can't think. I don't know what it is."

"Maybe he puts you under a spell. The way Dante in the circus does. Was that why you stood there as if you were paralyzed? Because he confused you?"

A rectangle of light suddenly fell on the ground.

"Momma's up," she said. "I have to go." And she hurried off as though my question had scared her away.

I walked out into the street. A couple in evening clothes were getting into a cab from a house diagonally across from us. Next to the door was the notions store with all its lights off. "What's the matter? Got an egg in your cap?" the lady in the store said to me once when I didn't take off my hat while I was shopping for Mom. "The hell with them," said Mom. "That's how people act in Ostermalm. As long as you say 'hello' in a nice way—that's all they care about."

I could tell just by looking in the street that the new term in school had begun. The second graders had found some chalk and scrawled all over the walls. With a few careful strokes, though, someone had changed all the dirty words into harmless ones:

141

PUCK, SHOT, TRICK. It occurred to me that Kossan had to be the one who'd changed them: whenever people started talking dirty, she'd turn her face and walk quickly away.

Had something dirty happened between Henning and Kossan? Maybe in his excitement or fear of the Black Knight he'd peed on himself? No, that would have been noticeable, people would have talked about it. So what else could have happened?

Dimly, I suspected that something had happened between them in the arena. And whatever it was, Kossan felt that she'd let him down. That's why she was willing to try to repair her error whatever the cost. As far as Henning was concerned, however, he belonged to the race of conquerors and commanders; he just took it for granted that soldiers and horses are loyal and true and will fight to the death for his victory.

20

Every time Kossan changed into a horse was just as strange as the first time.

She would stand there, patient and quiet, freckled and stocky with those light blue eyes of hers, while we unwrapped the material; the next moment the costume would swallow her up and a horse would be standing before us. Kossan and her costume had merged into a strange human-horse which we couldn't help but respect.

Henning held the reins gathered in his left hand; in his right he'd hold the lance. The right rein he placed between his thumb and forefinger, and he let it run out between his ring-finger and pinky. After a few afternoons he could direct her with a few small flicks of the reins; she learned to depend completely on him and to keep her eyes on the ground. When Max and I went up against them we didn't stand a chance of keeping up with their quick maneuvers. A twitch of the reins by Henning, and she'd turn on the spot—while Max had to scream and shout: "Left! Right! Stand still!" They worked together so closely, so much like a machine, that it was almost spooky.

"Isn't it horrible to have that bit in your mouth?" I asked, and Kossan shook her head.

"No. Just the opposite. It helps me feel like a horse and react like one."

Gradually, Henning prepared for the battle. The first goal, he said, was to "get a technical advantage." No doubt the Black Knight would have a shield, but it wouldn't be anything like Henning's, which was made by a real soldier, a warrant officer who did odd jobs for the general. It was made out of a sheet of tin plate, and it was completely impervious to lance points. It bulged slightly outwards so that the blows against it would slide off more easily, explained Henning. On the inside was a leather strap through which he could stick his arm. This time he wouldn't wear a helmet but an old fencing mask which had a light metal grid that concealed his face almost as well as an ordinary cloth mask.

Finally, either he or the warrant officer had fitted the lance with a hand-guard to protect his hand from his opponent's lance; it also gave him an even better grip.

All this time we kept to the outhouse above the washroom in the part of the yard that was hidden from view. When we took a break, Kossan would lie down on all fours, but she didn't scrape or clown around the way Nils-Wilhelm's horse had done— she'd simply rest. We'd sit with our backs against the yellow plaster facade of the building; the sun would warm us, but the fall shadows kept creeping up to us. I'd close my eyes and listen to the preppies' quiet talk; the sharp blows of carpet-beating in the adjacent yard; the clear, shrill cries of children; and in my mind I'd imagine that I was in the warm heat of Spain. I tried to think of why—was it a book I'd read, a film? No, it was a phrase about Don Quixote, the Knight of the Mournful Countenance, *on* the Mournful Countenance: it was one of the preppies' sardonic phrases that had stayed in my mind.

"The Black Knight comes in," Henning said to Max, "and what does he see? Not Kossan—whom he's been expecting—but an unknown horse who looks solid and strong, a knight with an impenetrable shield, a lance with a hand-guard, and a fencing mask which covers 100 percent of his face."

"If only Kossan doesn't lose her grip! With that shield and everything, you're going to be plenty heavy!"

Henning had to admit that it was a weak point— even if Kossan practiced with the special "training sack" that Henning had made. He squatted by the wall, thinking, and drew diagrams in the ground. Then he looked at Kossan; the horse head lifted itself as obediently and attentively as Tarzan did with Ken Maynard.

145

"We could tie her hands together. Then she wouldn't lose her grip even if I got hit hard. Or if the Mute tried to push her and knock her off-balance. Max, run up and get your skate laces."

With Henning on Kossan's back we tied her hands together with the laces and tightened them. She shook her head and said in a muffled voice:

"Harder! Like that! That's right!"

Kossan trotted around the little square arena. The tin shield glistened, and Henning tried different positions with the lance until he was satisfied. The one problem for him was to get down; Kossan had to kneel so that he could climb out of the grip of her bound hands.

"That's good!" he said, pleased. "Now she can't let go. We've got the victory in the palm of our hands. We'll get the whole thing set up the day before the tournament—but now I've got a lot of grammar homework to do!"

We put the equipment away in the empty outhouse which we'd locked with padlocks. When we took off the horse head, Kossan was completely soaked with sweat.

"It's warm today," said Max. "And this is thick cloth, the kind they use for winter coats."

In another stall we'd put Kossan's training sack, a gunny sack filled with trash, rags, and broken bricks. As she toddled around with it on her back in the dimness, she looked like a crazy kind of Santa Claus.

"Stuff a little more into it," Henning said to her.

"And practice stopping short and making very quick complete turns. It's possible that the Black Knight won't go down after the first time I hit him. The Mute is tough."

While she went obediently over to the stall, the rest of us went down the stairs away from the faint outhouse smell. Some sheets were hanging out to dry on the outermost lines like a protective white wall. At the very moment we came around the corner of the backhouse, Rebecca and Buffalo Bill walked into the yard.

"Hey, where are you guys coming from? What are you up to?" Rebecca asked immediately.

My heart started to race; it felt wonderful that she was here, close to me.

"Just over in the next yard. We climbed over the wall and down on the roof of the old outhouse," Max answered.

"You look guilty. What kind of tricks are up your sleeve?"

"Tricks are your specialty. I see you've got my book with you. Better than *The Condor*, right?"

Buffalo Bill had news. The battle between Henning and the Black Knight would be first on the bill before the revenge-rematch between the Grand Street Knights and the Nameless Knights.

"Some of the guys are in a hurry. They're going to be in the Air Defense Games at Gardet. But they don't want to miss you."

"No, but you know who might miss it?" said Rebecca. "Me! Buffalo Bill's thinking of charging double entry. Just because it's *à outrance!*"

"No little kids are going to be allowed in this time. You horses can sit on the steps and see the show while you're waiting to go on." He turned to me when he said this. "And you can only attack on the left, on the shield side, or else you'll be disqualified. And you have to hit the shield."

We were standing under the oak tree. The shadows had begun to creep up even further. Buffalo Bill was a little nervous about the bare weapons: did Henning have a good shield? Cardboard wouldn't do.

"What does it look like?" said Rebecca. "Show us."

"It's two meters wide and made of the finest oak," said Max.

"I told everyone they're not allowed to laugh at Kossan," said Buffalo Bill.

"If I'm still going to use Kossan," said Henning.

Buffalo Bill and Rebecca looked surprised.

"But who else could you have?"

"Don't worry. It'll be someone from the yard."

"Aren't you the mysterious one! But don't underestimate the Black Knight. Remember what it says in *Ivanhoe:* 'Beware! the Devil is on the loose,'" said Rebecca, who seemed slightly bothered by the secrecy.

"Well, honorable gentlemen and beautiful ladies, I'm off to my piano lesson," said Buffalo Bill. He'd managed to work the hefty music book down into his coat pocket.

148

"And I'm going for my screen test," said Rebecca, throwing her arms out and looking at the sky. "Aren't any of you going to see *Santa Fe Trail* this Sunday?"

"Lovey-dovey films!" said Henning contemptuously.

"Richard Arlen!" said Max, equally contemptuously.

Rebecca looked at me, a strange look, amused and flirtatious, and I got warm all over and mumbled something about maybe going, but I didn't know if she heard me.

"That stuff about Kossan was good," said Henning after they'd left. "We've got them going. This will confuse them even more. They'll have no idea who's hiding under the horse head."

Santa Fe Trail! Every Sunday around 11:00 Olle and Sixten and I would meet to do our usual routine, but this Sunday I'd already half-decided to go to the Rex on Odin Street and see *Bandit Trail* with Gary Cooper. Now they'd have to go without me. *Santa Fe Trail* with Richard Arlen! Ugh! But the look she'd given me was unmistakable.

Later that evening, around twilight, Kossan was doing her training rounds by the outhouse. I shouted commands to her: "Stop! Turn right! Back up!" It gave me a terrific feeling of superiority and satisfaction to see how blindly she'd obey every order.

The evening was unusually cool, but Kossan sat down next to me completely dripping with sweat.

149

"You should wear something warm when you take a break," I said. "That's what athletes do. Otherwise you get stiff."

"There's some material in the sack."

She picked at the rope the sack was tied with but couldn't get it open.

"I'll run up and get a blanket."

I had a grayish purple blanket with checks on it which I'd inherited from Grandpa. When I went upstairs and took it from the box under the kitchen bench, Mom looked questioningly at me.

"We're practicing now. Henning's going to fight the Black Knight from the Deepest Darkness," I said.

"Oh," said Mom as she stood by the stove. As long as you said something, it hardly mattered what.

"The Deepest Darkness?" said Pop.

He was making a sewing box from a blueprint in *Allers*, a ladies' magazine. Over the last few years he'd grown farsighted, and he wore glasses when he had to do close work. They were the old-fashioned kind you just pinched on your nose, and he looked curiously at me over them. "Nobody knows what it means," I said, crumpling up the blanket under my arm.

"The hell they don't," he said. "Long ago, several hundred years ago, there was a toll stake down near Narva Avenue. Probably once there'd been a toll gate where Gumshorn Street is now. And whatever was on the other side of that stake people used to call 'the Deepest Darkness.' They thought that decent people shouldn't go beyond that stake."

150

So it was that simple. And Pop had known something that none of those educated preppies had. That is, if you could believe him. Sometimes I discovered that both he and Mom said completely incorrect things off the top of their heads as though they were God's truth.

"Maybe it means that the Black Knight comes from around Gumshorn Street," I said to Kossan. "But that doesn't really help us too much."

She was lying on the ground using the sack as a pillow. I spread the blanket over her. In the twilight her face looked pale and shiny.

"Roland the stable boy," she giggled.

The blanket was long. I thought of pulling it over her head and face and saying something about the sun going down. But I stopped myself: Grandpa had the same blanket on him when he died after spending two bedridden years at home.

He'd been a ship's carpenter in the Navy, and he got a pension from them every month which Mom took care of. We didn't even discuss putting him in an old people's home: "Then they'd get the whole pension," she'd say.

So she looked after him herself. His legs couldn't carry him anymore, and even though sometimes she managed to get a pot under him, most of the time he did everything in the bed. That was why she was always washing and drying sheets and towels. Now and then an old guy came to give him a haircut, and sometimes, when he had a fever, a doctor came.

"Ask Grandpa if he wants a cup of coffee," Mom

said one evening around ten. I went in to ask him. He was a little senile, but sometimes he improved, and then what he'd say would make sense. This time I thought he looked strange; his eyes stared unseeingly straight up at the ceiling. I called Mom.

She saw at once that he was dead, and she began to cry. Poppa put on his jacket and went to get the doctor.

"Poor Grandpa," Mom sniffled. "Maybe it's just as well. But we won't get the pension anymore."

She closed his eyes and straightened his arms. Then she pulled the blanket over his face. Poor Grandpa. Poor, poor Grandpa.

"Why are you doing that?" I asked.

"That's what you do when people die," Mom answered absently. "The face doesn't belong to us anymore."

21

The Sibyll Cinema was right behind the National Theater.

That was where I'd seen *The Man in the Iron Mask,* and it was the greatest movie experience of my life. Only D'Artagnan, the last of the Musketeers, was left, and there was this evil villain hiding behind a drapery who stabbed him in the back with a dagger. But to fool the cardinal, D'Artagnan pretended that he wasn't mortally wounded; he dragged himself slowly out of the room, and only when he was out in the clear did he collapse. Boy, did I cry!

"That happens a lot with knife wounds," said Pop afterwards when I'd told him about the film. "All you feel is a little prick, a sharp twinge that's over in a few seconds. Then bang, a little while later you fall down dead. Internal hemorrhaging. That's what happened to a buddy of mine, Big Billy, down in Malmö. He went home for lunch and he said all of a sudden,

'Hey, I feel lousy,' and he fell flat on his face and died. Some carpenter's apprentice had slashed him in the factory. He's probably still in the clink."

Most of the people who were interested in *Santa Fe Trail* were girls, some with little brothers and sisters in tow. Normally I wouldn't have paid money to see such a movie. By instinct we knew when there was lovey-dovey stuff in a film, and *Santa Fe Trail* was one of them. So at first it burned me to waste my good money on Richard Arlen. But when I thought of that look Rebecca had given me—well, that made me change my mind completely.

It was getting late. Rebecca hadn't shown up yet. First it was 1:15, 1:20, then 1:30. The lobby was empty, and still no Rebecca came sauntering down the little dead-end street. I started to imagine that in some mysterious way she'd managed to avoid me or come so early that she was sitting in the theater wondering where *I* was.

So finally I went in. I sat way in the back. After the short, when the lights came on, I wandered slowly down the aisle. Still no Rebecca.

After the movie was over, I felt miserable. Typical of women to fool you; the same thing happened in the film. And after I'd gone to so much trouble with my big sisters saying, "Hey, will you get a look at Roland! He's plastered his hair down with water, and he's actually put on a clean shirt! You wouldn't be going out on a date, would you?"

Our house was on a corner, and there was a special

kitchen entrance on the sidestreet through which you could also enter. The people who lived in the backhouse could use either that entrance or the front door. Usually I didn't use the main entrance, but this Sunday I did; I didn't feel like describing *Santa Fe Trail* to Kossan who was probably standing in front of the "little door" (that was what we called it) waiting for me. What an anticlimax—to to tell the film to Kossan instead of talking it over with Rebecca!

I opened the heavy front door. Before me was an elegant staircase with rugs on the floor and marble on the walls. To the left a magnificent oak door to the apartments in the front house, and to the right a simpler wooden door which led to the yard and the backhouse.

Just as I was going through the hallway someone called. "Roland!"

There, standing by the oak door, was Rebecca! She frowned:

"I couldn't go to the movies. I had to go with my mother and father to Max's! Relatives!" she moaned. Even she had to follow her parents' orders. "So how was it?"

"It was good!" I lied.

"Sit down and tell me about it."

We sat down on the windowsill half a flight up.

That's what I liked about her: she took the initiative, and that showed you she liked you. And so as I told her about the film, I became more and more animated; I moved my hands and mimicked the actors, and she watched me attentively.

"You tell it well," she said, sounding surprised.

"I usually describe movies to Kossan," I said, the blood rushing to my cheeks.

"Max said that Kossan is going to be a horse again," she said.

"He told you? But it was supposed to be a secret!"

"I'm his cousin! And anyway, why should it be a secret? Everybody will be able to see for himself the minute they come into the arena."

"They won't know it's Kossan. She has sort of a mask."

"A mask? Max didn't say anything about that. That's clever! Is it a black mask like the Black Knight's?"

"It's . . . it's a secret," I said hesitantly.

"Roland! You and I don't have any secrets between us, do we?"

She nudged me playfully and looked at me with her luminous eyes. There was something so soft and charmingly open about her. Sometimes in the evenings I'd think Kossan away to make room for Rebecca: in my mind she'd see me and come slowly towards me, and we'd sit silently on the stairs feeling each other's closeness. We'd feel completely connected to each other without having to say a word.

Rebecca noticed my hesitancy, and she added:

"Roland! Max is my *cousin!* I'm practically part of this yard!"

"She's . . . she's going to be dressed like a horse," I stammered.

"A horse? That's wild! That's really wild! Oh, Roland, you've got to tell me. I promise I won't tell another soul! Cross my heart and hope to die!"

Her luminous eyes seemed completely sincere. She took my hand and pressed it to her mouth to show me how silent she could be. Her lips were slightly parted; the tip of her tongue darted out between them and touched my palm for a second. My ears buzzed, my palm tingled wonderfully; I got terribly excited.

"She has a horse head," I said in a thick voice. The secret will bring us closer together, I kept saying to myself. Her eyes glittered, she still held my hand in hers and coaxed me: "A horse head? A horse costume! How interesting! How very interesting!"

As I told her about how Henning was trying to build up a technical advantage, she listened intensely.

"A tin-plated shield! Brilliant! That's something the Black Knight probably hasn't thought of. I bet he's got one of those clumsy wooden shields that's awkward and difficult to handle. Is Henning going to have something written on it? And a fencing mask— he'll be completely invulnerable! . . . And what a great idea to tie Kossan's hands; he'll never fall off! . . . Is she a good horse?"

"She says she *is* a horse. She becomes totally different when she puts on the horse head and the costume."

Rebecca looked thoughtfully at my hand. Her face

157

was so serious, as if she were thinking over everything I'd said.

"You have hands like a pianist, Roland. Long, narrow fingers with beautiful nails!"

It seemed to me that while she was speaking, she was thinking about something else. But I sat with my mouth open—nobody but Mom had ever said anything about my hands, and all she'd said was, "Wash your hands, you pig!"

"It's probably the same way with the Black Knight," she continued. "When he puts on his mask, he changes. That's why he's so dangerous; he feels anonymous, impervious. Don't you think that's why people have costume parties? They can hide behind the masks and do things that they wouldn't ordinarily do. Awful things—because in a way it isn't they who are doing it. It's like that magic helmet in *Siegfried: mist and darkness conceal me!* . . . though it isn't the body that's concealed but the everyday self. Henning will see. Who knows what dark powers the Black Knight will have when he fights Henning to the death?"

A door opened higher up on the staircase. Laughter and talk.

"I better go now."

She bounced to her feet, once again sparkling and lively. Touching me lightly on the cheek, she went upstairs. I wandered outside into the yard as if in a fog, completely drunk. It was so different from the way I felt when I thought about the "0" model Erector set; this feeling was richer, fuller, more powerful.

158

Pictures of Rebecca whirled in front of me—closeups of her face, perfectly bronzed and smooth with sunny eyes; her narrow fingers, the cascade of dark hair; and long shots of her straight back and the lithe way of walking, her slender legs and her way of sticking her hands in her jacket pocket which gave her a roguish, Dead End Kid sort of look.

I was so excited that I spun around my bough and climbed way up into the tree; I just couldn't sit still!

A while later Kossan came out in the yard. When she saw me she looked disappointed.

"How did you get in?"

"I dropped out of the sky, of course. Then I walked right through the door."

"But I was outside the whole time waiting."

I explained that I'd gone through the front door. I was just about to tell her that I'd met Rebecca, but it felt almost sacred; I didn't want to give up the slightest part to anyone else.

"What movie did you see?" she asked, and she wanted to hear all about *Santa Fe Trail.*

"It was lousy," I answered, and in a mocking, cynical tone of voice I told her all about the oily Richard Arlen and his romantic problems. As she sat listening eagerly, something occurred to me: I was exactly like Mom. With Kossan, I told the truth, I didn't make anything up or change anything. But with Rebecca who came from a rich family, I was willing to lie about the movie; I knew she wanted it to be good, and I couldn't disappoint her.

22

It was a grand sight.

Henning sat in full battle regalia on Kossan, a dark brown horse whose hands were bound tightly with straps so that she couldn't let go of her rider. He was wearing his gold costume with his left arm through the leather strap of the shield, which was painted gold and red with a jagged line in between; it protected his whole left side down to his thigh. In his left hand he held the reins, in the right the lance whose sharp point glistened in the sunlight. His face was unrecognizable behind the fencing helmet's metal gridwork.

Max and I were speechless with admiration. We were so moved that we laughed uncontrollably, and we were warmed by the thought of how upset the preppies would be when the Black Knight was unmasked and Kossan's horse head lifted off. Kossan! they'd all shout and applaud; and our revenge, our triumph, would be complete.

We'd hung Kossan's training sack on a clothesline. Henning lunged at it over and over; sometimes he'd twitch the reins to the left and Kossan would swerve quickly in that direction; and sometimes he'd pull the reins back and she'd stop so short that her blue sneakers smoked. The sack swung slowly to and fro, pierced by the lance point many times.

"Perfect!" said Max, clapping his hands. "You'll knock the Black Knight out of his saddle with one shot tomorrow. But for God's sake, don't tire Kossan out!"

Almost reluctantly, Henning got off. We untied the straps around Kossan's hands and took the horse head off. She was soaked through but she shrugged it off—"It's just a little stuffy in there," she said. "It's nothing."

"I probably should have used some thinner material," Max said. "But this thick stuff really looked like horsehide."

We put away all the things in the outhouse almost as though we were having a ceremony. The stuff that Max would use as a Nameless Knight was already in there, and now Henning put his equipment in an empty box in a neat and meticulous way, put the horse costume next to it and covered everything with his shield.

Silently we stood behind him. I halfway expected that he'd make a speech or say a prayer before battle like Gustaf II or the Karla Street Knights. I started saying to myself, "Henning the Famous Fighter . . ." But all I could think of as rhymes were "lighter" and "tighter," and they didn't sound very elegant.

After Henning and Max went upstairs to their homework, Kossan and I stayed down by the stairs to the outhouse. I looked up at the blue sky. I felt the same nervousness I felt before a school outing: would the weather be nice?

"Did you see," said Kossan, "how Henning put my horse costume under his shield?"

"You want to walk on stilts a little?" I suggested.

Kossan rubbed one corner of her mouth; it looked like the bit had left a mark. On a few occasions when she'd been wearing the horse costume and she'd adjusted the horse head so that it merged into her brown-covered arms, there was something familiar about her, something I'd seen before. Suddenly it dawned on me what it was—she looked like one of the pictures in *Gulliver's Travels* when Gulliver is in the Kingdom of the Horses—a Houyhnhnm who stood on his back legs and held both his front hooves in front of his face as he threaded a needle.

When I told her that, she lit up. (With Kossan, when she was happy it didn't surface immediately the way it did with Rebecca. It started slowly, filling not just her face but her whole body; she got softer, warmer, it was a change you could actually feel.)

"The Kingdom of the Horses! Oh, yes! That's where the horses are the crown of creation and the Yahoos are dumb animals even though they look like human beings. I loved it when Gulliver was there. Do you remember what the horses said? That it was against reason to give girls a different upbringing from boys, because that was how girls—who made up half the world—become incapable of doing anything but having children."

"I must have skipped that garbage."

"It would have been so fantastic to be in the Kingdom of the Horses! They didn't even have a *word* for lying. Can you imagine, that's how inconceivable it was!"

"I'm sure Henning would love this," I said pointedly. "Kossan, the crown of creation, and Henning, a dumb Yahoo."

We walked over to the abandoned outhouse where we kept the stilts. Kossan walked behind me; the floorboards squeaked. She was still in the Kingdom of the Horses; she said in a low voice, as if to herself:

"The Kingdom of the Horses! One day we horses are going to go over the ocean the way Gulliver did and leave the land of the Yahoos. And we'll get them to stop fighting, we'll abolish war, and nobody will have to be at the bottom of the heap. We'll take control and there won't be any words for lying, for rich or poor. No word for rich, no word for poor, no word for violence, no word for war—they'll be totally unknown!"

23

Finally the day of the tournament arrived.

The September morning began as gloriously warm and sunny as the others, but by the middle of the day, for the first time in a long time, large clouds drifted in. Even so, it was still warm, breezeless and muggy—people said that a thunderstorm was on the way.

Henning hadn't wanted to carry all the battle equipment openly through the streets, so we wrapped it in brown paper; Max came up with a whole roll, probably from some paper maker who hadn't been able to pay the interest.

"There's going to be a concert during the intermission," he told us. "A harmonica trio."

"Just as long as they all play the same tune," said Henning.

"Maybe people will throw money down to them the way they do to the street players. That would be neat."

164

Kossan and I walked a few steps behind the two preppies. I carried the lances, one of which we hadn't wrapped up. Kossan lugged a heavy package containing the helmet and the horse costume. When we arrived at Maiden Street, we stopped in a doorway on the other side of the street, and Henning sent Max across to see if all the knights and horses had arrived; he didn't want anyone to see Kossan and the equipment beforehand. Max brought his brown battle tunic, his helmet and his lance to stow behind the curtain.

We waited. The narrow street was almost empty. Next to the worn outer door through which Max had gone was a bag factory; a few bales of paper were stacked in front of the place like huge dice. Close to us there was a second-hand bookstore, and Kossan and I looked at the books but we couldn't concentrate and we ended up chattering to each other.

"Today maybe they won't throw as much money to the horses because they had to pay double to get in . . . Pop has this big harmonica which he takes out sometimes. I could get one so the two of us could play in the street . . . Do you know it's Henning's turn to go in first?"

"But it won't be like the last time," she said. "Now I'm a real battle horse."

She smiled—quickly and shyly—a butterfly-light smile that was almost imperceptible.

Max returned and reported.

"It's totally packed in there. They're almost sitting on each other's shoulders. Everybody's there . . . that is, everybody but us!"

We crossed the street and went in. Up on the landing I peeked out through the painted door to the arena. My fellow horses were sitting on the stairs curled up against the railing. And what a crowd of faces up on the top of the wall! And such noise and laughter and conversation—it was just like a real stadium!

"Eight minutes to go," said Max, and closed his watch case. "Give us a hand, Roland."

It was dim in there and we were nervous; we kept getting in each other's way.

"Don't be so clumsy!" hissed Henning, putting on his gold tunic. "You're putting the horse head on backwards!"

Finally Kossan was ready. Henning mounted. First I gave him the shield and then the lance. He stuck his left arm in the shield's strap and held the reins as Max tied Kossan's hands together with his laces.

"Is it too tight?"

The horse shook its head. Max patted the horse's nose; it looked funny. "Good horse," he said.

I looked out.

"Buffalo Bill's coming down the stairs!"

We all took a last look at Henning and Kossan; close up, they were frightening, overwhelming. Henning pointed the tip of his lance at us—"Get out!"— and we slipped out the door into daylight. Reluctantly, Olle moved to make room for me in the crowd while Max went up to the top of the wall. Sixteen gave me an anxious nudge.

166

"I heard some guy saying that the cops know they're fighting with bare weapons. Did you hear anything about it?"

"So what?" said Olle. "They have shields."

"But you can get a lot more power with a pointed lance," said Sixten. "In *Ivanhoe* the knights get hit so hard they go flying off their horses and break their necks."

As Buffalo Bill stepped to the center of the arena, the Boy Scout stood ready. The ground was very dry; little puffs of dust rose with every step Buffalo Bill took. He stood right in the center and raised his arms.

"Honorable gentlemen and beautiful ladies! I bid you welcome to the deciding match between the Black Knight from the Deepest Darkness and Henning the Noble, a brave and fearless knight. This will be a return match *à outrance*. The knights must aim exclusively at their opponent's shield; otherwise, the usual rules apply. May the best man win!"

In the arena the air was completely still. I looked up. The sky was overcast, iron-gray; it must have been stifling for Kossan in her thick clothes and horse head. As Buffalo Bill walked over to the brown door below us, the bugler climbed up on his blue and yellow box. He pointed his horn straight ahead and blew energetically—a blaring fanfare that bounced off the white wall, echoing and resounding like the sound of a hundred bugles.

Buffalo Bill opened the door.

Kossan glided out into the arena with a few long, quick strides. The moment Henning pulled the reins she stopped. Was it really Henning on Kossan? No, a mighty knight had turned his yellow and red shield towards us and pointed his long, sharp lance towards the sky. Above the gaudy shield we could see the metal mask which hid his features and the brilliantly eye-catching red collar. Kossan was completely possessed by her role as horse—every step she took was horselike, her head swaying back and forth, slightly raised, watchful, attentive. First there were surprised "oohs" and "ahhs" from the preppies, then a strong round of applause. My fellow horses were all talking at the same time; they were as excited as the preppies.

"This one beats Nils-Wilhelm by a mile! The Black Knight doesn't have a chance!"

"I hope they get it over fast—then we can take on the Nameless Knights!"

"Hey, you guys, he's got reins. Did you see he's got reins?"

"What kind of disgusting mask is *that*?"

"Look at the horse's hands! They're tied!"

"What a shield! You could *never* break the damn thing!"

During this time Buffalo Bill crossed to the cellar door on the other side of the arena. He had to wait for a long time before the preppies turned their attention from Henning and Kossan; they stood stock still, apparently enjoying the sensation they were causing.

Finally Buffalo Bill fished the big key out of the hidden pocket in his ringmaster's cape and stuck it in the lock.

At the same moment the fanfare sounded; the Scout had turned his bugle to the cloud above us. The notes rang out and disappeared, plaintive and melancholy. He was good, that bugler—really good.

The door opened. The Black Knight made his entrance.

A strange murmur rose from the crowd, and I turned to stone. Before me they stood: the Black Knight and the Mute were dressed and outfitted exactly like Henning and Kossan—but all in black!

24

In the movies, the villains were always after the secret formula that would give their side complete control over the whole world. They didn't think twice about using beautiful girls like Mata Hari for spies, and the ambassador's right-hand men would always fall for these miraculous women and then give away all the secrets. I used to think of them as spineless jellyfish you couldn't help despising, but now I knew what it was like to be one of them—a traitor.

Rebecca had put her hand over my mouth—cross my heart and hope to die! And in spite of that she'd rushed right off to the Black Knight and told him about all of Henning's ideas. I was miserable—and jealous. It was the Black Knight she'd run to, it was he she'd been thinking about all the time! What devotion, what love! The kind of loyalty and limitless faith that I'd always dreamed of for myself!

The Mute was a black horse with a black horse

head which was possibly even more realistic than Kossan's. Thin leather reins—exactly like Kossan's. And the Black Knight had a fencing mask over his cloth mask, his left arm held a tin-plated shield like Henning's, and his black lance had a sharp metal tip and a hand-guard.

"They look exactly alike!" Olle blurted out, flabbergasted. "Hey, you guys, it's unbelievable! The Mute has got his hands tied too so that the Black Knight *can't* get knocked off!"

"Laissez aller!"

The bugle had hardly sounded before the two horses rushed towards each other. The knights sat hunched-up with their shields held close to their bodies. The horses were equally fast—they looked like they were going to run right into each other, nose against nose, at the arena's midline.

Both knights straightened up and pointed their lances towards their opponent's shield. The clash between them was tremendous—their lances crossed and hit the shields simultaneously. There was a jangling sound, and then came two sharp, dry, cracking sounds—the lances had split! The horses stopped themselves in mid-charge; both knights swayed backwards but didn't lose their seats. The Black Knight recovered his balance first; frantically he thrust his broken lance at Henning, the splinters from the lance flying all around him. The sheer savagery of his attack surprised Henning, who couldn't get his shield back up.

At the top of the wall the preppies were howling like madmen. Olle screamed.

"Hit him again! Get him down!"

Kossan faltered. Suddenly Henning relaxed the reins and she stumbled towards the cellar door, looking for a moment as though she were going to fall. The Mute came trotting towards us. The Black Knight's lance was broken at the hilt; with an impatient motion he threw the worthless weapon away and turned the Mute back to the field with a light tug of the reins.

This was the first time we'd had a chance to see the front of his shield. It was painted black, and across it "The Angle of Death" was written in white letters.

A mixture of applause and booing from the top of the wall.

"The Angle of Death?!" said Sixten. "He's got to be one of us—he can't spell either."

Over by the cellar door Henning had also thrown away his broken lance. He pulled the fencing mask off and let it fall to the ground. Running his hand through his blond hair, he seemed to shimmer in his gold costume as he picked up his shield and shouted across the arena:

"Black Knight! It's shield against shield—or else consider yourself defeated!"

The Black Knight followed Henning's example— he loosened his fencing mask and threw it to the ground. Without saying a single word he raised the black shield menacingly toward Henning. Up on the edge of the wall they were still buzzing; the excitement of the first violent clash hadn't died down yet.

"Did you see the Black Knight's shield?" said Olle. "There's a big dent in it just where Henning hit it!"

"The Black Knight kept going at Henning even though the lance was completely shot," said Sixten. "The splinters were flying like a thousand arrows!"

On a signal from Buffalo Bill the Boy Scout brought the bugle to his lips—a short, defiant signal to begin.

The Mute was noticeably quicker this time, and it looked like Kossan was almost collapsing under Henning's weight. Both knights held the reins in their right hands and moved the shields around to get the best grip. Henning looked firm and resolute; he raised Kossan's drooping head just as he collided with the Black Knight.

The shields met with an echoing, metallic clang. The horses butted each other, and the knights hit each other's shields with furious intensity.

Gradually, however, it became clear that in this kind of intense infighting, Henning was the heavier and stronger of the two. Twice he came close to knocking the Black Knight out of his saddle, and you could feel that the rejoicing was just about to start. But one of the times Kossan hadn't had the energy to take the last step which would have clinched the whole thing, and the other time the Mute's bound hands prevented the Black Knight from falling off.

173

The Black Knight was on the defensive. As blow after blow fell, he hunched deftly behind the shield and pulled the reins—the Mute backed up, and little by little they came closer to us and the low wall.

Suddenly Henning pulled the rein hard—Kossan's mouth must have hurt—and Kossan swung rapidly around; there was great strength behind Henning's fierce blow, and with a clanging sound he hit the Black Knight's shield squarely. The Black Knight cried out; the arm with the shield flew up, and he himself was pushed backwards. The Black Knight hit the ground hard on his back, and he lay with his shield over his head and the Mute at his feet.

An earsplitting cry of triumph rose from the preppies—then a blaring bugle fanfare.

The Black Knight had finally been defeated! As Henning lifted his shield proudly toward the people on the edge of the wall, Kossan's knees folded under her. She sank on all fours to the ground, and because of that looked even more like a horse than before; it seemed comic that it happened just as Henning was raising his shield in triumph. But he freed himself quickly from her tied hands and whispered something to her. She's just wiped out, I thought; it had been only in the last seconds that Henning had gotten the advantage over the Black Knight!

Henning took a few steps towards the Black Knight. He lifted the shield off with one gesture—in spite of the Black Knight's resistance—and pulled off the long hood and mask which covered his face.

174

"Who is it? Who is it?" the preppies screamed.

First a cascade of dark hair, then a familiar face.

Rebecca!

"Rebecca! Rebecca is the Black Knight!"

He stared at her.

"*You're* the Black Knight?"

"*Give me my mask!*" she screamed, struggling to her feet. She was was so angry that she clenched both fists and started hitting him. "Goddammit! I should have got a new lance! Goddamn Henning, I was supposed to *beat* you! That was the point of the whole thing! To show you damn pompous preppies that a girl can beat any boy!"

"A girl!" said my friends sitting next to me.

"The Black Knight was a girl! How weird!"

The preppies streamed down the stairs and out into the arena. They surrounded Rebecca and Henning and picked up the shields, tried the fencing masks, collected the pieces of the lances. We on the staircase were pulled along with them; I ended up next to Kossan, and I poked at her with my toe.

"Hey, Kossan, get up!"

Max appeared at my side.

"Rebecca! Who would have believed it! She acted so innocent! And she was the Black Knight all along! . . . What's the matter with Kossan?"

"She's just tired," I said.

"She's really become a prima donna! She's used to us dressing and undressing her." He sat on his haunches next to her and untied the laces around her hands while I pulled off the horse head. Her face was totally pale and dripping with sweat; at the corner of her mouth was a red bruise.

There was an incredible commotion in the arena—feet and legs all around us—and the dust was like a cloud, like a battlefield. Everybody pushed and buzzed with so much enthusiasm that we could hardly hear what Kossan said.

"It's . . . she searched for a word, and at the same time put her hand to her left shoulder ". . . sharp here."

Max put his hand inside the neck of the costume. "Ahh!" Kossan cried. He pulled his hand away—his fingers were completely red, and his eyes grew big and round. Uncomprehendingly he studied his hands; he thought that somehow he'd hurt himself without feeling any pain. Finally it dawned on him where the blood was coming from.

"Henning!"

Strangely, as though he'd been prepared for it, Henning heard his voice in spite of the commotion. When he came over followed by Buffalo Bill, I moved away with the horse head in my hands. Max held up his red fingers for them and nodded at Kossan. It felt good to see how concerned they were.

"What is it?" said Buffalo Bill, bending over her.

"A long splinter from Rebecca's lance, I think," Max said. "It went through the costume and under the collar-bone."

He wiped his hand on Kossan's brown-covered leg.

176

Henning also crouched on his haunches next to her; in his costume, he looked like a figure out of a legend. When he put his hand under the poncho the same way Max had, Kossan opened her mouth, but no sound came out. He looked up at Buffalo Bill:

"She's bleeding!"

"A lot?"

"A hell of a lot! Call an ambulance! Tell the super. Hurry. Say that there's been an accident. Give me something to stop the bleeding with."

Kossan's face was chalk-white. Her eyes darkened, became black. She seemed so scared that it hurt *me* and I would have given anything to free her of that vast, lonely fear that was taking control of her.

"It's only to be absolutely safe," said Henning, çalming her.

"Yeah, it's like when you get hit by an Indian arrow," said Max. "You know that you shouldn't try to pull it out until you get to the fort and the doctor can take it out. Otherwise you'll bleed to death."

Gradually her eyes became almost normal again. "I don't . . . need an ambulance," she said, trying to sit up. But Henning wouldn't let her, and Max pulled the cloth tubing off her arms and legs.

25

It was only when the two men from the ambulance came in behind Buffalo Bill carrying a stretcher that groups of preppies noticed that something had happened.

"What is it? Oh, Kossan. Yeah, she's lying over by the stairs." They all crowded around her, and the men had to push them away to make space. After a quick examination they lifted her up and put her on the stretcher.

"It was an accident," Henning said.

"It couldn't have been me," Rebecca cried out. "Absolutely not!"

The men looked wonderingly at them; Henning and Rebecca still had their battle costumes on. Then the men lifted the stretcher and went towards the door as the obliging preppies held it open.

Out on the narrow street there was suddenly a group of people; an ambulance was an Event. Who was sick, who'd had an accident, who was dying, who was having a baby? The windows in the building flew open. All the preppies left the arena—big, curious packs who pushed us horses aside, though Olle said angrily: "She's our Kossan." It was exciting to know someone who was being taken away in an ambulance.

"It's a Chevy," said Sixten contentedly. He was a Chevy man. The ambulance had a big red cross in a white circle on its side; the back doors were wide open. The men picked up the stretcher and put it in the bunk to the right. To the left were two ordinary chairs behind each other. The two men jumped down and talked with Henning and Max. Some grownups were now mixed into the crowd, and no one seemed to be in any hurry. I couldn't see what was going on; there were too many preppies in their school caps between me and the van. But then I noticed that I was standing next to the bales of paper from the bag factory, and I climbed up on them so that I could see over the crowd and into the ambulance.

Kossan lay with her feet facing inside. Her head with the fuzzy red hair rested on a pillow. Over her they'd put a gray blanket with purple stripes on the side.

Finally the men finished talking. One of the ambulance men climbed in and sat next to the bunk, turning towards Kossan. He looked down at her. The other, the driver, shooed away curiosity-seekers and closed the left-hand door, the one closest to the sidewalk. All of a sudden the other man called him; the driver climbed in through the half-door. I could see their backs, how they were bending over Kossan. Then the driver hurried out again.

Over everybody's head, just as he closed the other door, I saw what happened. Once, kidding around, I'd said to Kossan that the Black Knight froze the blood in my veins and made the hair on my neck stand up—but that's exactly what happened now: ice in my veins and a strange, sizzling sensation in my hair!

The man inside the van had picked up the corner of the blanket and pulled it calmly and gently over Kossan's face; instead of dull red hair I saw a gray blanket. Mon's words came back to me: "The face doesn't belong to us anymore."

The ambulance drove away, honking a few times to get the bicyclists and spectators out of the way. I stood alone, paralyzed. Some raindrops fell; I'd almost forgotten what rain looked like. Henning and Max, Buffalo Bill and Rebecca stood in the street surrounded by the other preppies. Rebecca lowered her head; she looked sad. She stood between Henning and Buffalo Bill, and it was Buffalo Bill who comforted her by putting his arm around her shoulder.

That business with the blanket, I thought. It didn't have to mean anything. And like a confirmation came my friends' voices under me:

"They didn't have the siren on. It wasn't anything

serious," said Sixten. And Olle added: "Probably just a little loss of blood. She'll be back in school tomorrow. Girls are as tough as chewing gum."

It had to be true. Soon she'd be back in action with her little kids and jump rope and teacher games, and I'd be teasing her about the books she'd borrowed.

Kossan.

One day Max had called down to us from his room facing the courtyard. For one time in his life he was all alone—no cook or maid at home. He shouted down that the first person to get to his room would get some special Swiss chocolate; the second one would too, so we did it just for fun.

Kossan and I tore up the stairs, but she was quicker on the turns and I stumbled and followed after. When I got to the fourth floor she was standing next to a door ringing the doorbell for all she was worth. She was expectant and happy.

"Hey, what are you doing? Max doesn't live here. It's one flight more!"

She looked at the nameplate on the door, and her face turned completely red. We could hear heavy steps inside, and I whispered, "Come on! Let's get away before they come!"

But then came that singlemindedness of hers again: you had to take responsibility for what you did, and so she waited for Mr. Bergstrom, Bank Manager, even though she was so nervous she was shaking. She curtsied and stuttered an apology:

"I . . . I rang the wrong bell!"

"You didn't have to ring it so damned hard," said Mr. Bank Manager Bergstrom and he slammed the door in our faces.

It was an insignificant, ridiculous episode, but I saw it vividly in my memory right now. I saw her burning red cheeks and tremendous embarrassment, and I felt the same feeling of pride I'd felt then. She had real class. I saw her standing in front of Bergstrom's door and casting a frightened glance in my direction. I'd felt endlessly sorry for her then: why hadn't I changed places with her and taken the brunt of Bergstrom's nasty words? Suddenly tears filled my eyes when I thought of her frightened and lonely look.

Below me my friends started to get restless. They wondered out loud how the return match would go between the Grand Street and Nameless Knights.

"Buffalo Bill says there's not going to be any more tournament!" someone said.

"No more dough? Won't they do it ever again?"

"Where's Roland?"

I realized that I was still holding Kossan's horse head in my hands, and I put it on for the first time.

The world disappeared; it grew completely dark.

"Look, Roland's turned into a horse!" said Sixten.

"We've got a new Kossan," said Olle.

As though I were looking through a prism, I peeked out through the slits in the horse head. I took in Kossan's sweat, her smell. And Kossan's voice still echoed in the horse head, and I could hear her calling from the abyss:

"One day we horses will travel over the Seven Seas like Gulliver and we won't carry the rich and powerful on our backs any more. We'll take control of our lives and everybody will have the same opportunities and the same rights in our kingdom, the Kingdom of the Horses, and there won't be any words for lying or deceit, no words for violence or war, no words for rich or poor."

"Come on, Roland," said Sixten.

"Can't you see it's not Roland, it's Kossan!" said Olle.

Carefully I climbed down from the paper bales without taking off the horse head and joined my fellow horses.